A Protector for Phoebe

Love will OUT #2

D.E. Haggerty

Copyright © 2021 D.E. Haggerty

All rights reserved.

D.E. Haggerty asserts the moral right to be identified as the author of this work.

ISBN: 9789083349435

A Protector for Phoebe is a work of fiction. The names, characters, places, and incidents portrayed in it are the product of the author's imagination. Any resemblance to actual persons, living or dead, events or locations is entirely coincidental.

All rights reserved. No part of this publication may be reproduced, stored in a retrieval system, or transmitted, in any form or by any means, electronic, mechanical, photocopying, recording or otherwise, without the prior permission of the author.

No portion of this book may be reproduced in any form without written permission from the publisher or author, except as permitted by U.S. copyright law.

Also By D.E. Haggerty

A Hero for Hailey
A Soldier for Suzie
A Fox for Faith
A Christmas for Chrissie
A Valentine for Valerie
A Love for Lexi
My Forever Love
Forever For You
Just For Forever
Stay For Forever
Only Forever
Meet Disaster
Meet Not
Meet Dare
Meet Hate
Bragg's Truth
Bragg's Love
Perfect Bragg
About Face
At Arm's Length

Hands Off
Knee Deep
Molly's Misadventures

Chapter 1

Step 1 – Throw the rules for being a lady out the window ~ Phoebe's rules for becoming a better person

I GIGGLE AS I watch Hailey's fiancé and father play tug-a-war with her. I startle and look around to see where the sound of laughter is coming from. Surely, it's not me. I may be laughing more since I took a job with Hailey, but it's not an everyday occurrence. Heck, it's not an every week occurrence. At least not yet. But things, they are a changing.

"It laughs!" My friend, co-worker, and klutziest girl in the world, Suzie, proclaims before jumping from her chair. She raises her hands in the air and promptly smacks the person next to her. "Oops!" is all she says as she dances away. I should add she's also completely oblivious.

Suzie and Hailey own the PI firm, *You Cheat, We Eat,* where I'm currently interning to become a private investigator. I still can't believe it. Me? A PI? I'm sure stranger things have happened, but I wouldn't know what.

Slightly more than a year ago, I'd never even held a job before. And now I'm doing my best to become a private investigator.

Maybe I should have started with something a bit easier than PI, like say telephone receptionist, but Hailey and Suzie didn't ask questions about my background or why I needed a job despite my fancy clothes. Plus, they pay me in cash. I couldn't say yes fast enough.

Suzie returns and grabs my hand. "Come on. We need to congratulate Hailey."

Hailey's boyfriend, Aiden, proposed to her tonight in front of everyone. Sigh. It was super romantic. Hailey is a total drama geek, so Aiden made us all dress up in Regency era clothing à la Jane Austen time. He was supposed to propose like Darcy proposed to Elizabeth in *Pride and Prejudice*, but Hailey kept correcting everything he did apparently, she's not only a drama geek but a drama perfectionist. Eventually, he gave up and dropped to his knee.

Suzie drags me to the stage where Hailey is standing with a smile stretched from ear to ear on her face. Suzie jumps on stage and since she refuses to let my hand go no matter how much I protest, I find myself on the stage as well. My heart starts to pound. I do not like being the center of attention. Especially not now. I scan the room, but no one is looking our way. Phew.

"Congratulations!" Suzie shouts and tackles Hailey. Suzie is a munchkin at a mere five-feet-two, but she has no problem taking down Hailey despite the woman being half a foot taller than her. I manage to disentangle my hand in time to remain on my feet.

"I'm happy for you!" Suzie shouts and Hailey cringes. Suzie has one volume – ear shattering loud.

Aiden comes to his fiancé's rescue. He hauls Suzie to her feet before helping Hailey up and pulling her into his arms.

I clear my throat. "Congratulations, Hailey. I'm happy for you." I may no longer believe in love and marriage and all that icky stuff, but I *am* happy for her. Aiden is the perfect man for her, and she's been crushing on him for decades. She deserves her happily ever after.

Plus, Aiden is a total hottie. At six-foot-three with dark hair and olive skin, he looks like he stepped off the cover of a romance novel of some Greek holiday romantic tale. Of course, Hailey is no slouch in the looks department either. She's always complaining about her lack of boobs and bootie, but her lithe body makes her look like a dancer despite her uniform of ripped jeans and shitkicker boots. How anyone manages to look graceful while constantly wearing chunky boots is beyond me, but she does.

"Oh." Suzie rubs her hands together. "We should drink champagne to celebrate. I'll get some." She rushes off forgetting she's on an elevated stage. Instead of taking the steps down, she walks right off the edge and ends up face down on the floor.

Hailey sighs and starts to move to her friend. I stop her with a wave of my hand.

"I got her."

By the time I've walked down the stairs, Suzie is already back on her feet.

"What happened?" she asks as she looks around in a daze.

"You decided you can fly. Big surprise. You can't."

Her mouth drops open. "Were you snarky with me?" She sniffs and places a hand over her heart. "Our girl is growing up too fast. Before you know it, she'll be off chasing boys and drinking at frat parties."

Jokes on her. I will not be chasing boys ever again. Nope. The male gender is nothing but trouble. As for frat parties? Been there. Done that. Except for the drinking. Nope. Drinking is for 'men and boys, not ladies'. Lord forbid if I were to act unladylike.

We walk to the bar where Hailey's uncles have congregated, although 'uncles' isn't technically correct. Lenny, Barney, Wally, and Sid are Hailey's dad's Army buddies. They helped raise Hailey since her mom took off when she was twelve years old. Is it wrong I envy Hailey for not having a mom around? Yeah, probably.

"What's the difference between a wife and a job?" Barney, the self-proclaimed funny guy of the group, asks. "After ten years, a job still sucks." He guffaws and raises his hand for a fist pump. I wrinkle my nose at his fist. Do I look like the kind of woman who does fist pumps?

"Change the word wife to husband and I'm with you," I mumble under my breath at a volume no one can hear.

Suzie's eyes widen as she looks at me. "Have you been married, Phoebe?"

Oh crap. It's never good to give Suzie a hint about my previous life. The woman is positively obsessed with figuring out my past. I stare her straight in the eyes and lie. "No." Thanks to my past she's dying to know about, I'm an expert in lying.

"Oh." She frowns. Yep, my lying skills are unmatched.

Before she gets a chance to ask more questions, I announce I need the facilities. Lucky for me, Suzie is not the type of woman who insists on going to the restroom with her friends. I try not to run as I escape down the hallway to the restroom where I hide in a stall.

Phew. That was a close call. I need to learn to keep my big mouth shut. It was easy enough when I first met Hailey's family. Her uncles and her dad are super intimidating. I don't know what they did in the military, but their body language screams *don't mess with us.* I needed no reminder to keep myself to myself. But as I've gotten to know them, I've realized they're all a bunch of big old teddy bears. Teddy bears who can kill a man with their bare hands, I remind myself.

I repeat my mantra to myself several times. *I am Phoebe Adams. I am a strong woman. I am a survivor.* Once I've said the mantra enough to convince myself it's true, I stand and exit the restroom.

I walk down the hallway with my head bowed, my mind full of all the things Hailey has to look forward to. Things I will never have. Marriage, children, happiness. I threw those things away. Well, not the happiness part. My past and happiness do not belong in the same sentence.

Too busy wallowing in self-pity, I miss the man standing at the end of the hallway, blocking the entrance to the bar. I run smackdab into him. "Oh, sorry," I say and try to move around him.

His hand grasps my upper arm to stop me. "Phoebe, isn't it?"

A shiver runs down my spine at the sound of his deep voice. I look up and gasp. Shit. Shit. Shit. This man is dangerous. I can feel it. I met him a few months ago when he approached me at the bar and asked for my name. When I told him my name was Phoebe Adams, his eyes narrowed in disbelief. I was convinced I'd been found out, but I haven't seen the man since. I thought I was in the clear. I guess I was wrong.

"Um, yes." I clear my throat. "And you are?"

"Ryker," he grunts.

The name Ryker fits him to a T. He's tall – way taller than me and I'm five-foot-nine. He must be at least six-six. He's also wide as a linebacker. And it's all muscle, not an ounce of fat to be seen on this man. His long-sleeved Henley is pulled taut over his chest and stretched to the limit on his biceps.

He's handsome in a rough, outdoorsy way. He sports a scruffy, dark beard, and his hair is a bit long and out of control, as if he couldn't be bothered to waste any time on it. My eyes land on his and I swallow before I can gasp. They are bright, mossy green and I swear they can see right through me.

My body warms and I nearly stumble when I realize I'm interested in this man. I haven't been interested in any man in such a long time I barely recognize what the warming in my belly means.

"Can I help you?" I ask after I wrestle my hormones into control. I am cool and collected. I am the ice queen after all.

"Yeah." He leans closer. "Do you want to go out with me?"

Go out with him? Whether I want to or not is immaterial. I can't go out with him. If there's one thing I've learned in life, it's that men cannot be trusted. Which is why I've sworn them off, except for book boyfriends. Book boyfriends are the only boyfriends in my future. I look up at him, determined to tell him no, and my body starts to tingle from the heat in his eyes.

"I …"

Suzie comes barreling around the corner. I never thought I'd be excited to see her.

"This is a private party. What are you doing here?" She's a foot and half shorter than him, but she has no problem getting right up in his face. I should take lessons from her.

"My mistake," he says with a shrug. "I'll see you around." I'm not sure if his words are a threat or a promise.

Suzie watches him leave. "Wow. The man is h-a-w-t. Hawt." She fans her face. "You should totally go to bonetown with him."

Go to bonetown? I've never taken a trip to bonetown. Don't get me wrong. I'm not a virgin, but bonetown sounds like way more fun than I've ever had in the sack. Unfortunately, I will not be going to bonetown with him or any other man. Sigh. My life sucks.

"Come on." I put my hands on her shoulders and steer her toward the bar. "Let's get you a drink to celebrate."

At the word drink, Suzie forgets all about Ryker. I shudder. His name is as sexy as the man himself. I better not see him again or I'll be in trouble. And I'm already in enough trouble to last a lifetime.

Chapter 2

If you decide you want to become a kickass PI, do not wear dry clean only clothes to work. ~ Phoebe's rules for becoming a better person

I STUDY THE BORING beige suburban house. According to the case file, Stan Brown lives here. Except Mr. Brown is supposed to be dead. Supposedly, he was killed in a work-related accident. I flip through the file as I keep one eye on the house. Brown is a highway construction worker who 'died' when a car smashed into a barrier he was standing next to and went up in flames. His body was never recovered. Shiver. How horrid.

Well, it would be horrid if it were true. Because Stan Brown is apparently alive and well and living in suburbia. Due to rumors, the man was planning to fake his death, the insurance company is dragging its feet paying out the widow. But so far, no one has been able to prove Brown is alive. *You Cheat, We Eat* is the third investigative firm the insurance company hired.

I never thought I'd be working at a place called *You Cheat, We Eat,* but I have to admit I kind of love the name. Hailey says since she makes most of her money chasing cheaters, she might as well advertise the fact. Plus, there's no better way to get revenge on cheating men than by making money on outing them.

I don't chase after cheaters, though. When Hailey and Suzie agreed to take me on as a future investigator, we decided I would concentrate on insurance fraud cases. Apparently, I'm not inconspicuous enough to chase cheaters. Yeah, right. In my old life, I was practically invisible.

But wearing the clothes of my previous life makes me stick out in my new life. Yeah, yeah, I get it. The Furstenberg wraparound dresses and Louboutin high heels are a bit over the top. But those are the clothes I owned. I wasn't going to throw an absolute mint in fashion clothing away just because I ran away from my old life. Instead, I brought it all to my new life. Except the clothes make me stand out like a blinking road sign in my new life.

Suzie claims you could wrap me in clingwrap, and I'd still stand out. She's the queen of exaggeration. Yes, I'm five-foot-nine and I've got the requisite curves. Unlike Hailey, I was first in line when boobs and bootie were handed out. But I've spent my life starving myself to ensure those curves don't go out of control. It's hard to appreciate your body when you're always hungry.

In addition to my curvy body, I'm blonde with green eyes. I think my eyes look exotic with a slight slant to them, but according to my mother, I'm one in a million blonde-haired girls. There's absolutely nothing special about me or so she's told me a million times.

I shut thoughts of my mother down. Thoughts of her will lead to thoughts about the rest of my loving family. Sarcasm intended. Thinking about my so-called family is akin to jumping the fast train to depression. Been there. Done that. Have the bruised heart as a souvenir.

I lean my head against the headrest and force my eyes to stay open. This is my third day of surveillance on Stan Brown's supposed house and I am bored, bored, bored. Hailey warned me when I begged her for a job that being a PI was boring. I should have listened. What am I saying? I still would have taken the job.

I straighten when I hear an engine. Is Brown finally leaving his home? The garage door hasn't moved an inch in the past three days. *Come on, come on.* I cross my fingers and zero in on the garage door. It doesn't move. Darn. My shoulders drop and I sigh.

A delivery van passes. Ah, that explains the engine noise. I watch as the driver slams on his brakes halfway down the street. The obnoxious beeping sound delivery vans have when reversing starts up and the vehicle backs up the street.

When the van stops right in front of the Brown residence, I squeal and pull out my camera to start taking pictures. As the delivery man slams his door, I keep my camera trained on the front door of the house and wait for someone to open it. Fingers crossed it's Stan Brown.

The door opens and a woman steps out. Darn. Not Stan then. I take several pictures anyway. I zoom in to get a closer look. The woman resembles Melanie Brown, the widow. At least I'm at the right house. The delivery man approaches dragging a trolley holding the world's largest television. How in the world does the widow of a construction worker have the money to afford such an obnoxiously sized television?

Melanie ushers the delivery man in. Before she slams her door, she scans the neighborhood. Huh. In my experience, you want your neighbors to know when you've bought a big-ticket item. Bragging rights and all. Melanie's behavior is more than a bit suspicious.

I need to take action. Sitting on my butt in a vehicle parked outside of the Brown residence for days on end isn't going to prove Stan Brown is alive and well. And I don't get paid unless I get the proof. I hook the strap of the camera around my neck and exit the SUV. I start tiptoeing down the sidewalk but stop when I realize I look suspicious, not to mention stupid, tiptoeing in broad daylight down an average street in suburbia.

I casually stroll around the block instead until I'm standing near the Brown's backyard. A fence surrounds the yard. But this is not some charming white wooden picket fence. No, this is a privacy fence clearly designed to prevent peaking into their backyard and back windows, which is strange since this is suburbia and no one else has a fence around their yard. Considering it also looks brand-spanking-new, my suspicious radar is on high alert.

Since the temperature is around freezing and there's a light snow falling, no one else is out and about. Perfect. I look around one more time to make sure I'm truly alone out here. Yep, I'm all alone. Everyone is probably tucked up in their homes where it's cozy and warm while I'm outside discovering why people flee the Midwest for the West Coast. The wind whipping off the lake sure is cold in this city.

I study the fence for a moment. I'm guessing it's higher than six feet, maybe seven. I'm five-nine, I can totally do this. All those stupid gymnastics classes I was forced to take as a teenager are finally going to come in handy. I take a running leap at the fence and grab the top. My legs flail for a moment, but I manage to get traction and haul myself over.

I land on my feet inside of the Brown's backyard. For a moment, I have the urge to throw my hands in the air as if I just landed a double layout with a full twist. A feat I never managed in my short gymnastics career. I squash the urge and kneel down. I see a hedge and maneuver myself behind it to get my bearings.

Once my heart rate is back under control, I peek out from behind the hedge for a look at the house. My jaw drops. This side of the house does not look like the boring beige suburban ranch the front does. Not at all. The entire back wall is windows, and the ceilings are vaulted. On one side, there's a kitchen to die for with marble countertops and stainless-steel appliances. On the other side is the open living room where someone is installing a television nearly as large as the wall.

My suspicious radar is now beeping in the red alert area. There is no way Melanie Brown can afford this house. Unless she happens to be expecting a great big paycheck from say an insurance company.

I slowly make my way to the other side of the yard, camera at the ready, with my eyes fixated on the house. My foot slips and I look down to see I've walked onto a tarp. A tarp? Why is there a tarp in the middle of their yard? I scan the area and realize the tarp covers an inground pool. Oh shit. I stand perfectly still, wondering if the tarp can handle my weight. My feet begin to sink. I guess it can't. I leap toward the edge of the pool. The tarp collapses before I can reach safety.

Suddenly, I'm waist-deep in water. I grab the camera and hold it above my head as I slog my way to the stairs now visible in one corner of the pool.

"Hey! Get out of my yard!" A man shouts.

There's no need to yell, I'm leaving already. I take a running leap at the fence and vault over it. As soon as my feet land on the other side, I'm moving. I run as fast as my feet will take me to my vehicle. I don't take time to catch my breath once I'm inside. I switch on the engine and tear out of there.

I keep my eyes peeled on the rearview mirror as I fly out of the suburb. When I don't see a vehicle chasing me, I slow down and crank the heat up. I am absolutely freezing. Being drenched in thirty-degree weather will do that to a woman.

By the time I park in the underground parking garage of the building where the private investigator offices are located, my teeth are chattering. I may have managed to keep most of my coat dry, but my pants are soaked through as are my cheap canvas shoes. At least I wasn't wearing my Louboutins.

I squish my way to the office, dripping water all over the place as I go. I open the door and Lola, Hailey's dog, immediately rushes out of Hailey's office and comes barreling toward me. This dog loves me. Way too much if you ask me. I push her snout away.

"Not today, Lola."

"Look what the cat dragged in." Suzie points to me and cackles.

Hailey rushes out of her office. She slaps Suzie on the shoulder. "Stop it. Phoebe looks frozen. What happened?"

My teeth chatter as I open my mouth to answer.

"Never mind. Let's get you warmed up. I have some sweats in my office. They'll be a little short on you, but they're clean and dry." Hailey's an inch shorter than me, but at this point, I'd take a pair of pants from a munchkin as long as they're dry.

Lola lays down in front of me with her big head on her paws and whines. "I thought you were getting her fixed."

"Poor Lola. The mean lady wants to get you spayed." Suzie pouts and claps her hands for the dog to come to her. Fat chance of Lola obeying when I'm around. I'm not bragging. The dog is scary obsessed with me.

Hailey shoves sweats and a pair of fluffy socks into my hands. "Go, get changed."

I don't argue despite never having worn a pair of sweats a day in my life. Even when I was doing gymnastics, I wasn't allowed sweats. I could wear a warm-up outfit but sweats? Sweats are undignified and unladylike. Never mind I was a fourteen-year-old girl.

When I come out of the tiny restroom of our office, Hailey and Suzie are waiting on me.

"What happened?" Hailey asks while Suzie rubs her hands together in anticipation.

"Coffee," I demand. Since we don't have a coffee maker in the office, my demand should buy me some time.

Suzie holds out a to-go cup. "I know you like plain black coffee, but I got you a pumpkin spice latte. I figured you could use the extra sugar."

I don't like plain black coffee. Does anyone? Plain black coffee is bitter and boring, but it also has zero calories. Pumpkin spice latte probably has five-gazillion calories, which is five-gazillion minus twelve-hundred too many. I don't complain, though. Since I don't have money for fancy coffee, I'll take whatever I can get.

"The Browns have a pool," I start and then go on to tell them about my embarrassing day.

Hailey taps her chin. "Maybe we should tell the insurance company we came up with bupkis. Two other firms couldn't find any evidence Mr. Brown faked his death either."

My nose squishes of its own accord. I do not want to admit to failure. I've had enough of failure in my thirty-one-years of living. I clear my throat. I don't like disagreeing with Hailey, but I need to start standing up for myself. It's about time someone stood up for me.

"I'd like to give it one more try."

Hailey shrugs. "It's your choice." She stands and returns to her office like it's totally no big deal I contradicted her. Maybe it's not?

Suzie claps. "If this is the result of you continuing to try, I'm all for it." She gives me two thumbs-up.

I roll my eyes and head to my office. *My office.* Just thinking the words fills me with glee. I know I'm not bringing in enough business for the firm to merit my own office. Not yet, I remind myself. Because I am bound and determined to become the best darn PI *You Cheat, We Eat* has ever seen.

Chapter 3

When in doubt, take a bow. ~ Phoebe's rules for becoming a better person

I STARE AT THE sign as I stand frozen on the sidewalk – McGraw's Pub. The bar Hailey's dad – aka Pops – owns and runs has become my second home since I moved to Milwaukee. Second home? Scratch that. I've never had a home before – at least not one where I felt welcome. But I do feel welcome at McGraw's.

Then why I am standing frozen on the sidewalk? It's all the uncles' fault. Since I started working for Hailey, Lenny, Barney, Wally, and Sid have 'adopted' me. Which, on the one hand, is awesome. No one has actually *wanted* me to be a member of their family before. But – and this is a big but – they are the most overprotective men to walk the earth.

When they find out I took a nosedive into a swimming pool today, they're going to go apeshit. They are not happy with my decision to become a PI. They think I'm too soft-hearted. Hah. They have no idea. There is not one thing soft about my heart.

Suzie skips to me and asks, "Watcha looking at?"

"Nothing. Clearing my mind is all." I'm such a liar.

She snorts before grabbing my hand and yanking me into the pub. The woman doesn't know what boundaries are, let alone that the word 'no' exists in the English language. Her name should be menace.

"Here she is! The winter diving champion!" she announces when we enter the bar.

I glare at her. And, yes, I know glaring is unladylike, but I don't care. Being a lady never got me anywhere except to Heartbreak Alley. A place I'm determined to never visit again.

Barney and Sid whistle and clap. There's only one thing to do. I curtsy. Since I'm wearing a tight sweater dress, the movement isn't as elegant as it should be. No one seems to mind as the rest of the bar patrons join in on the clapping. Despite knowing it's all in good fun, my face warms. My first big case and I end up in a swimming pool in November. I keep my head bowed to allow the heat to dissipate.

Hailey and Aiden rush in behind us. Judging by the mess of her hair and the look of satisfaction on Aiden's face, they've been enjoying each other's company if you know what I mean. Of course, Suzie notices as well.

"Someone got a hole in one." She raises her hand to high-five Hailey who frowns at the hand. She rolls her eyes before wiggling her still raised hand in my direction. I shake my head. I don't do high-fives. And if I did, I wouldn't high-five to celebrate events in someone's sex life.

In my previous life, sex was never talked about. Never. This life is different, however. Suzie doesn't shy away from making rude comments. And the uncles? They're always trying to one-up each other with dirty jokes. And Hailey is an active participant. Right in front of her dad!

"What's the difference between a G-spot and a golf ball?" Barney shouts. Barney is the worst. He never met a bad joke he didn't like. It doesn't matter how dirty it is and whether there are ladies about. Oh wait. I'm not a lady anymore. I'm plain old Phoebe Adams, soon-to-be PI.

Barney doesn't wait for anyone to guess the answer. "A guy will actually search for a golf ball." He guffaws and Suzie skips over to him to give him a fist bump.

Lenny approaches and wraps an arm around my shoulders and squeezes me tight. Damn. His arm around my shoulder squeezing me tight sure feels good. Not in a sexy way, although Lenny is hot for an old guy. Suzie calls him a DILF despite him not having any children.

"You doing okay, Doll?"

I smile at his question. Before I arrived in this city, no one bothered asking me if I was doing okay. If I had a frown on my face, Mom would be all like *'You're creating wrinkles. Stop frowning!'* I guess I should be happy she noticed. No one else did.

"I'm fine." I'm not lying. Well, maybe a teeny tiny lie. I will be fine. And, let's face it, nothing bad happened except my pride took a bruising. Since pride is the deadliest of all sins, the root of all evil, I'm going to ignore the bruising and motor on with my life. Thus, I'm fine.

"Are you sure you want to be a PI, little one?" Wally asks. Where Lenny asked because he takes being overprotective to the nth degree, Wally is pushing because he thinks I'm in over my head.

I asked Hailey about Wally once. Her response? You don't want to know. Of course, now I'm super duper curious. The man could give lessons on how to be secretive. He goes off on these 'trips' and no one knows where he is, what he's doing, or how long he'll be gone. He calls it 'going off-grid'. I call it suspicious.

"I'm not little." I wave a hand over my body. I'm five-nine without heels. And, except for when I'm investigating an insurance case and falling into swimming pools, I'm almost always in heels. Today, I'm wearing my brown leather boots with a three-inch heel, putting me at an even six-foot. I tower over most men. But not Wally, unfortunately.

Sid joins our huddle. "Why don't you find yourself a good man instead of working your fingers to the bone?"

I roll my eyes. "Not happening."

Sid is a diehard romantic. He's been married several times. He also resembles a blond Norse god. I'm thinking Odin, the supreme deity and the greatest among the Norse gods – the Allfather of the Aesir. I may have a little obsession with Norse mythology. I blame Chris Hemsworth and those Thor movies. Movies were my escape in my previous life. And what better way to escape than watching Chris Hemsworth flexing his muscles. Sigh.

Pops joins us and pushes his buddies out of the way. "Leave her alone. Phoebe can be whatever she wants to be." He winks before handing me a vodka martini.

Pops is the best. The whole package. Hailey lucked out with him as her father. Sure, her mother took off when she was twelve, but knowing what I do about mothers, it was no loss. Too bad Hailey still struggles with abandonment issues. Poor Aiden had to work his butt off to get her to say yes to marrying him. But that's a whole other story.

While Pops goes back to tending the bar, the uncles move toward 'their' booth. It doesn't have their name on it, but it might as well have. They practically live there every night.

"Come on, tell us what happened." Barney rubs his hands in anticipation. "How did you end up in the pool?"

"You mean Suzie the big mouth didn't tell you?"

"Hey! I don't have a big mouth."

I snort. "Yeah, sure. And rainbows fly out of your butt."

She frowns. "We've created a monster."

At hearing her call me a monster, I flinch. I know she's teasing but old habits die hard. Wally's gaze zeroes in on me. Damn. The man misses nothing. What is he? Some secret spy? I give him one of my patented sure-to-make-a-man-drool smiles. He isn't buying it. He frowns, and I look away. I obviously can't win a staring contest with Mr. Super Secretive.

"Anyway." I clear my throat and take a sip of my martini before telling everyone about my adventures in backyard swimming today.

Everyone laughs except Wally. He tilts his head and studies me. "Why do you think Stan Brown is living there?"

I raise my hand and count off. "One, his supposed widow is definitely living there. I got her picture today." I pat myself on the back. I may not have gotten the money shot, but no other firm has managed to capture a picture of Melanie Brown yet. "Two, no woman needs a television that big."

"What's the deal with oversized televisions and men anyway?" Suzie asks the table. "Is this part of the whole misunderstanding about size? Because I've never met a man who knew what six inches was."

Hailey smirks. "I know how to measure six inches."

"Six inches?" Aiden raises his brow. "Pretty sure it's more than six inches."

Hailey rolls her eyes. "I didn't say it was six inches. I said I know how to measure six inches."

Wally clears his throat. "What else?"

"When I was … 'swimming'… a man shouted for me to get out of his yard."

"Maybe Melanie has herself a new man." Sid wiggles his eyebrows.

I'm not buying it. "Why haven't I seen him enter or leave the house then?"

"Maybe—"

Judging by the grin on Sid's face, I don't want to hear what he has to say. I hold up my hand to stop him. "I've staked the place out at various times throughout the day. No one has come or gone from the house. It's not normal."

Sid grunts in agreement, and I smile. Maybe I am good at this investigator stuff after all. I should be, considering how many lies and cheats I was exposed to in my previous life.

Pops arrives with a huge tray of food. My mouth waters as he sets plates of hamburgers and fries in front of everyone. With a wink, he grabs a bowl of tomato soup and places it in front of me. I force myself to thank him. I know there's no tomato soup on the menu and Carol the cook made it special for me since I try to keep to a healthy diet, even now when money is scarce.

Before I get a chance to dive into my tomato soup I wish was a burger, Hailey nudges me. "Check out Mr. Hottie making eyes at you."

I look over and sure enough, Ryker is sitting at the bar with his gaze focused on me. I feel my body heat. Is it hot in here? I feel warm. I fist my spoon to resist the temptation to fan myself.

Suzie leans across me to see who Hailey's talking about. "Isn't that the guy who asked you out?"

My blush intensifies. Did she have to tell the whole table? She nudges me with her shoulder. "You should tell him yes. I'm sure the trip to bonetown is still available."

Hailey reaches around me to smack Suzie upside the head. "Stop embarrassing Phoebe. If she doesn't want to date Mr. Hottie she doesn't have to."

"Damn right she won't date him." Lenny points at Aiden. "At least not until we get a background check."

Aiden shakes his head. "Not happening."

Hailey's fiancé is a police detective, which came in super handy when Hailey landed herself a stalker. But it's not handy when the uncles are up to their old tricks.

Wally snickers. "Like we need your help."

I ignore the uncles and Aiden as they argue about when it's appropriate to run a background check. They can run all the background checks they want. It doesn't matter. I'm not dating Ryker of the deep, growly voice or anyone else for that matter. Men and romantic relationships have no place in Phoebe's new life.

Chapter 4

Never make assumptions. Especially about how much dogs love you. ~ Phoebe's rules for becoming a better person

ANOTHER DAY. ANOTHER STAKEOUT. This time I'm prepared. I plugged my telephone into the car stereo and I'm listening to a podcast about self-empowerment. If there's one thing I've learned in this life, it's that you can't rely on anyone but yourself. Until recently, everyone in my life was dedicated to ensuring I knew I was nothing but arm candy and a baby maker. Not anymore.

I munch on carrots as I watch the house. Like the previous times I've sat in the SUV a few doors down from the Brown residence, nothing is happening. This suburb is the very definition of sleepy. Of course, it's the middle of the day and everyone is probably working or at school. No ladies who lunch are to be found here. They don't realize how lucky they are.

Once I finish the carrots, I realize I'm thirsty, but I don't have a drink with me. On my very first stakeout with Hailey, she warned me not to drink while on a stakeout as bathroom opportunities are extremely limited. She's not wrong. I don't see myself squatting behind a bush to take care of business. The very idea is abhorrent. My nose scrunches in disgust.

Stop it, Phoebe. Stop being a snob.

Lunchtime comes and goes but still no movement at the Browns. How can anyone possibly stay inside this much? As far as I can tell, they're not even ordering much take-out. What can you do inside with all those hours to burn? They can't possibly be playing around in the sheets all this time, can they? Doesn't he need some recovery time? In my admittedly limited experience, men can't go, go, go when it comes to sex.

I wait another hour. If I don't make my move soon, the kids will be out of school and I'll have missed my window of opportunity. I tap my fingers on the steering wheel before pressing stop on my podcast. I can't sit here idle a moment longer. Besides, it's not a big deal. What could go wrong? It's not like I'm going to suddenly get amnesia and forget there's a great big pool in the middle of their backyard.

I slip out of the car and walk around the block. Since no one called the police on the crazy lady running through their backyard yesterday, I assume it's safe to take the same route as I did yesterday. When I reach the privacy fence, I glance around but I'm still all alone out here.

I make a run at the fence, place my hands on the top, and vault over it. What do you know? Those rusty gymnastic moves are improving after a single vault yesterday. My mother would have a heart attack if she knew I'm using my gymnastics skills to break into people's yards. I land in the Browns yard and immediately hunch down. I waddle to a bush and hide behind it.

I study the layout of the yard, which is what I should have done yesterday. There are bushes lining the fence on three sides. In the middle of the yard, the pool is once again covered. I guess I didn't ruin the tarp. Off the rear of the house is a cement patio, currently empty of furniture, although there is a grill under a tarp near the kitchen door.

Okay, I tell myself. I got this. The light in the living room comes on and I creep closer. I will not be the idiot who walks into the middle of the yard straight into the pool today. I stick as close to the fence as possible without having to crawl through the shrubs.

The door in front of the kitchen slides open and a man whistles. I bring up my camera and zoom in to take a picture. Is it Stan Brown? Have I found him? Is one fuzzy picture enough for payday? I creep closer as I click away.

A dog's head appears at the door and he barks. The large black face with brown snout looks left and right and then raises his head to sniff the air. I'm not worried. Dogs don't scare me. Not even rottweilers. They're good-natured dogs, despite their reputation as savage dogs.

"Go get 'em, Killer," the man I suspect is Stan Brown says.

Killer? Who names their dog Killer? I watch as the man takes one step onto the patio. Yes! This is definitely the money shot. I take another step forward as I snap away. Suddenly, the dog barks and starts running straight toward me.

Shit! I spin around and run full out toward the fence. A man bounds over the fence right before I reach it. I come to a screeching halt.

"Come on," he shouts. "Get moving."

Hey, wait. I recognize him. It's Ryker from the bar. What is he doing here?

"But dogs love me!" I shout as I run as fast as I can from the barking beast.

Ryker isn't going to test the theory. He grabs my hand and practically throws me over the fence. I go flying! Suzie might not be able to fly but apparently, I can. Luckily, I was an ace at the vault and manage to land on my feet. I don't nail the landing but no one's judging me now.

I can hear the dog snarling on the other side of the fence. Ryker better hurry his ass over here. I see a hand on the top of the fence and then he's there. At way over six-foot-tall, he makes jumping the fence look like a small hurdle.

He tags my hand and starts running. "We need to get out of here."

"Why? The dog can't jump the fence."

"No, but a man with a shotgun can."

My eyes widen and I look over to Ryker to see if he's serious. I trip and nearly go to my knees. He releases my hand and rights me before grabbing my hand again. We run around the block to a large black pick-up truck.

I put my hands on my thighs and bend over as I take deep breaths. I didn't realize I was out of shape. Of course, doing Pilates in front of my television or running like the hounds of hell are on my ass work two different muscle groups. Maybe I should add cardio to my workouts if being chased by rabid dogs is what I can expect when I'm a PI.

"What are you doing here?" I ask when I finally manage to gain control of my breathing.

Instead of answering, he clicks the button to unlock his truck. "Get in. I'll drive you to your SUV."

I narrow my eyes. How does he know where my SUV is parked? Well, it's not my SUV. It's a company vehicle I'm allowed to use during stakeouts, which is handy since I don't own a car. I did own a car. It's hard to escape halfway across the country without wheels after all. Sure, busses exist, but I don't think Greyhound would have approved of the amount of luggage I took with me when I ran away.

"It's cold out," Ryker growls. "You're trembling. Get in the truck before I put you in the truck."

I have no doubt he'd pick me up and shove me inside. "Fine." I huff and walk around to get into his beast of a truck.

Once I'm seated with my seat belt on, he fiddles with the ventilators until they're aimed at me and blowing hot air my way. When the hot air hits me, I realize I'm absolutely freezing. I put my hands practically on top of the ventilators to warm them.

"Why aren't you wearing gloves?" Ryker demands.

I've had enough of men demanding answers from me, but I'll let him slide since he saved me and all. "I can't take pictures with gloves on."

He shakes his head as he puts the truck in drive and pulls out of his parking spot. He's parked a block over from the Brown's house.

"What are you doing in this neighborhood?"

I'm not expecting an answer, after all, he's ignored all my previous questions, but this time he does give me one. "I'm a bounty hunter. I followed one of my skips to the area."

My eyes widen and I swivel in my seat to gawk at him. "You're a bounty hunter? How cool. You must have some great stories."

He grunts in response. I guess I won't be hearing any stories about him taking down a naked, oiled up man then. I'm not making stuff up. Hailey's fiancé actually arrested a naked man once, although Aiden didn't mention whether the guy was all oiled up. My imagination supplied that little tidbit. What? Chris Hemsworth is not the only hot body worth watching. Turkish oil wrestling is a thing.

Ryker pulls up next to my vehicle and stops. I take a deep breath, grab hold of my courage, and ask, "Can I buy you a drink for saving my behind?"

Despite wanting to forget every single thing my mother ever taught me, the good manners she drilled into me are too far embedded in my personality to be forgotten. It's an automatic reflex to want to find some way to properly thank him for saving me.

I expect him to say no. Instead, he grunts. "Sure. I'll follow you."

I bite my lip to stop my jaw from dropping open. He said yes! Butterflies explode in my stomach. Oh wait. I don't want a man. And I certainly don't want a man who causes butterflies to explode in my stomach. What have I gotten myself into?

Chapter 5

Babe is not an answer to a question. Just saying.
~ Phoebe's rules for becoming a better person

I GET INTO MY car and drive to McGraw's Pub. I don't want to subject the man to the uncles, but I don't know any other bars. I should have thought of my dismal knowledge of the area before asking if I could buy him a drink. In my defense, I've never asked if I could buy a guy a drink before. I'm in unchartered territory here.

I park the SUV and Ryker parks his massive truck next to me. When I open my door, he's already there holding out his hand. I look at his hand for a second before I take it. Sparks fly up my arm and through my body. I can practically see a sign flashing 'Danger'. I yank on my hand, but he refuses to let me go. I look up to discover he's smirking. Oh great, he knows the effect he has on my body.

What am I thinking? He doesn't have an effect on my body. It's the effects of an adrenaline dump is all. Never mind the effects of an adrenaline dump are usually fatigue and feeling drained and not sparks flying all over your body.

We walk toward the entry to McGraw's with our hands entwined. The more I try to pull away, the more Ryker holds on. His body is shaking.

I glare at him. "Are you laughing at me?"

"Yeah, babe. You're hilarious."

My eyes narrow. "Don't call me babe." It's such a throwaway term of endearment. I am done with those. Done and dusted.

He releases my hand to place his in the small of my back and guide me into the bar. And darn it, I like the feel of his big, strong hand on my body even more than holding his hand. What is wrong with me? I never have these kinds of reactions to men. There's a reason my nickname is Ice Queen after all. Hold on. My nickname *was* the Ice Queen. The Ice Queen is in my past and she better stay put there.

I look around the bar and nearly sigh in relief when I notice the uncles aren't around. Maybe they don't live here after all. We take a booth in the corner and the waitress approaches immediately.

"She'll have a vodka martini with Stolichnaya," Ryker orders on my behalf.

My brow wrinkles. "What are you doing? Stalking me? How do you know my favorite drink?"

"Babe," is his only reply. As if saying one word is a reply.

I open my mouth to berate him. It's bad enough babe is a throwaway term of endearment, but I will not tolerate a man not paying attention to my wishes. Not anymore. The Phoebe who let men run all over her is no more.

"Princess, give it a rest."

"Princess? I'm no princess." And I'm certainly not his princess.

Lucky for him, Pops arrives with our drinks. He sets my martini down in front of me but keeps his eyes glued to Ryker. "You okay, Phoebe?"

I know I should be annoyed Hailey's dad is acting like an overprotective bully, but my stomach warms instead. No one – absolutely no one – has been protective of me before, let alone overprotective.

"Yeah, Pops. This is Ryker. He saved me today."

"Saved you?" Lenny asks. "Saved you from what?"

I jump in my seat. Holy shit. Where did he come from? Does he have magical powers? I peer around him and notice he's joined by Barney, Wally, and Sid. Are they all graduates of Hogwarts?

"Did you guys apparate in here or travel by the Floo Network or something?" I ask as I look around for a fireplace and residue of Floo powder. So, sue me, I'm a huge Harry Potter fan. When your sole means of escape is in your head, you tend to read a lot and fantasy books are the best sort of escape.

"First people talk about an alien abduction day and now traveling by Floo network. I think I'm missing out." Barney scratches his head.

Sid smacks him. "She's talking about a book."

Pops, Lenny, Barney, and Wally gaze at him with their eyebrows raised. He shrugs. "I have kids. It's impossible not to know about Harry Potter if you have kids."

Lenny returns his attention to me. "Don't make me ask you a second time, Doll."

Geez. Maybe I was wrong about this overprotective thing making my stomach warm. "It was no big deal. A rottweiler was chasing me. Big guy here threw me over the fence."

Lenny growls. "You threw her over a fence?"

While I cower from Lenny's growl, Ryker is completely unaffected. He grunts. "It was the quickest way to get her out of danger." He notices me cowering in the corner and reaches out to squeeze my hand. "You're scaring her. Cut it out."

The uncles and Pops are on instant alert. "We're scaring her?" Pops snarls.

My eyes widen at the standoff between Ryker and Pops. Uh oh. Time to wade in. I say the first thing to pop into my head. "When did the Browns get a dog anyway? And how do they have a dog? They never let the poor thing out. I would have seen it. Some people don't treat their pets right."

"Not sure babying a Rottweiler is the 'right' thing," Ryker says.

"Taking a dog for a walk is not babying. Dogs need to be walked."

Uh oh. I let myself get distracted. Stupid. Because now the uncles have all pulled chairs up to our booth and are sitting around us. Don't get me wrong. I love the uncles. I have a huge extended family back home. No. Not back home. In my previous life, I had an extended family. But no one cared about Phoebe. Except for how they could use her to get what they wanted.

"What are your intentions with our Phoebe?" Sid asks.

I need to shut this down. "Um, guys, Ryker has no intentions. We're not on a date. I asked him for a drink to thank him for helping me close the case."

"Close the case?" Hailey pushes the uncles out of the way to sit down next to me. "Did you get a picture of Stan Brown?"

Suzie claps and starts singing *We're in the Money*. She's dancing as well, except the woman can't dance. No, her version of dancing makes her look like she's having a fit of some sort. She runs into Barney's chair and takes a nosedive into his lap.

"Glad you could stop by," Barney says as he rights her and puts her on her feet. He stands and sets her in his chair. "Stay."

"I'm not a dog."

"Speaking of dogs, where's Lola?" I ask. Where Hailey goes, Lola goes.

"In the kitchen, where else?"

"Lola!" Suzie shouts.

"What are you doing?" I hiss.

The Chesapeake Bay Retriever comes barreling out of the kitchen and runs straight to our group. She doesn't stop until she finds me and starts humping my leg. My face heats as the men chuckle.

"I told you dogs love me," I tell Ryker.

The corners of Ryker's lips tip up in an almost smile. "You showed me."

Aiden arrives and grabs Lola's collar. "Come on, girl. Leave Phoebe alone." Lola whines, but he doesn't give her a choice as he pulls on her collar. "And that goes for the rest of you as well," he orders.

"What?" Suzie looks around. "What are you talking about?"

Aiden motions to me and Ryker. "Leave them alone."

"Why? Are they on a date?" Her eyes round as she takes me in. "Are you on a date?" She squeals. "Pound town party of one!"

Hailey holds up a finger. "Put the pause on crazy for a second." She looks at me. "Did you close the case? Seriously?" I nod. She raises her hand to high-five me. I may be feeling awfully proud of myself, but I still don't do high-fives. I wave with both hands instead and end up looking like I'm doing jazz hands. I'm doing an awesome impression of a total idiot.

She stands. "I want to hear all about it tomorrow." She addresses the uncles. "Come on, break it up. Break it up."

"But I want to hear about how she got the picture now," Suzie whines.

Hailey grabs her arm and hauls her to her feet. "Too bad. You can't always get what you want."

Suzie pouts the entire time Hailey drags her away. The uncles stand. Each one glares at Ryker before winking at me and walking off. I wait until every last one of them has left before speaking.

"I'm sorry. I'm sure this isn't what you had in mind when I offered to buy you a drink to thank you for your help."

He chuckles. "It's fine, Princess. It's good you have family to protect you."

"They're not really my family."

He freezes. "They're not? Where's your family?"

I wave his question away. I don't talk about my family. My former family that is. "I don't have a family." Before he can ask me another question, I cut him off at the pass with a question of my own. "Are you from around here?"

"You're an orphan?" Ugh. Can he not see I don't want to talk about it?

"Not exactly," I hedge. "What about you? Where's your family?"

"Grew up in care."

My eyes widen. I've never met anyone who grew up in foster care. Before I hit him with one of the thousand questions rolling around in my head, his phone beeps. He mumbles sorry before grabbing it from his back pocket.

He frowns. "Gotta go. A skip is in on the move."

"A skip?" What's a skip?

He reaches over the table and tucks a strand of hair behind my ear before leaning over and kissing my forehead. "Sorry, Princess. Raincheck?"

My head bobs in agreement before I can remind my body we want nothing to do with men, and he saunters off. My eyes can't help but watch his very fine behind as he leaves.

Suddenly, I don't mind the nickname Princess anymore.

Chapter 6

When crazy comes calling, keep your eye on the door and lie through your teeth. ~ Phoebe's rules for becoming a better person

"Hey, Phoebe," Hailey calls before walking into my office where I'm writing up the report on the investigation into Stan Brown. "Good job with the Brown case."

I smile as my whole body warms. Getting praise from anyone – let alone a boss – is a new experience, and I like it. "Thanks."

"Anyway." She takes a seat in the chair across from my desk.

It's a miracle an extra chair fits in this office. In my old life, this room would have been a broom closet. I barely have enough room for my desk, my chair, and one visitor chair. But I do have a window and a door. I know Suzie eavesdrops on all my conversations, but at least I can shut the door and pretend to have privacy.

"I need to go out on a job, but there's a potential client coming in soon. Can you handle him?"

My smile widens. I haven't done any client acquisition yet. In fact, the Brown case was the first investigation I completed entirely on my own.

"You're sure? You don't want Suzie to handle it?"

Her eyes widen and she glances over her shoulder at the open door. She clears her throat before sitting up straight in her chair. "No, potential clients are handled by the investigators, not the business manager."

I hear squeaking before Suzie rolls her office chair to a stop in the doorway of my office. "Yeah, yeah, yeah. I heard you the first two million times." She crosses her arms over her chest and leans back before stomping her foot. The chair goes flying backwards and then there's a thud. "I'm okay!"

Hailey rolls her eyes before focusing on me again. "You sure? You'll be all alone."

"What am I? Chopped liver?" Suzie shouts.

"You know what I mean!" Hailey shouts back.

I giggle. Sometimes it's hard to believe they've been the best of friends since grade school. I try not to be envious of their relationship, but it's difficult. They have what I've always wanted. Close friends and close family where everyone accepts you for who you are. No one's trying to mold either of them into their perfect version of a lady.

Hailey stands. "I'm out of here. Good luck."

"Thanks," I say but luck has nothing to do with it. I'm sure I'll be fine dealing with new clients. After all, I practically have a doctorate in dealing with persnickety people.

I'm printing out the report for the insurance company when the bell over the outside door to the offices chimes announcing the arrival of a visitor to *We Cheat, You Eat.* I smooth my hand down my skirt and make sure my blouse is buttoned correctly.

I'm surprised my hands are shaking. I can't allow myself to show signs of being nervous. I'll be chewed up and spit out.

No. In my previous life, I would have been chewed up and spit out. This is my new life. A new life I'm creating all on my own. I take a deep breath to center myself.

Suzie appears at my door. "Phoebe, there's someone to see you." She winks. Why is she winking? Suzie winking never heralds good news in my experience.

"Mr. Havers." She steps aside. "This is our investigator, Phoebe Adams."

I stand and walk around my desk to greet him. When the man enters the room, however, I falter for a step. I quickly right myself and extend my hand. I can handle a potential client who's wearing a tinfoil hat. I blink to clear my vision, but the man is still wearing the handmade hat.

Mr. Havers steps into my office and his eyes dash around checking everything out before finally reaching forward to shake my hand.

"Please, have a seat." I motion to the chair before walking around my desk and sitting. "How can I help you today?"

"You're not one of them, are you?"

I paste a smile on my face. "One of whom?"

He leans forward and whispers, "The aliens."

"No, I can assure you I was born and raised in America." I pretend to misunderstand him, hoping he's not as crazy as he appears.

"Not a foreigner. An alien. You know from outer space." Guess the crazy ship has sailed and Mr. Havers has a first-class ticket.

"I am one-hundred percent, purebred human."

I try to make light of the situation. Hailey in no way, no how prepared me for crazy clients. I thought I'd be dealing with a bawling woman carrying on about her cheating husband. I don't have any experience with emotional women, but I've been one too many times to count. I could have dealt.

But crazies? I have no experience with people who let their freak flag fly. Well, except Suzie, but she's perfectly harmless. At least to other people.

"What about listening devices?"

I open my mouth to ask him if aliens use different listening devices from humans but stop myself. Instead, I lie. "I swept the place for bugs before you came myself." Never mind I have no idea what a bug would look like, let alone how you do a sweep for them.

"Thank you. I appreciate it." He exhales and relaxes in his chair.

"Now, what can I do for you?"

"I need you to find the aliens that abducted me."

I blink rapidly to stop my eyes from widening in disbelief. I guess I should have expected some outrageous alien abduction story when he walked in with the tinfoil hat. In my defense, I've never seen a man in real life wearing a tinfoil hat.

What do I do? Play along? Tell him I'm not a ghost hunter and ask him to leave? But I can't let Hailey down. She asked me to represent *You Cheat, We Eat,* and I will do my darndest to handle this the way I think she would. Except I have no idea how Hailey would handle crazy guy.

"Why do you need me to find them? Wouldn't you rather forget all about the incident?" And by forget, I mean stop pretending you were abducted.

He squirms in his seat. "They have something of mine."

I'm almost afraid to ask, but I'm too curious not to. "What do they have?"

"My sperm."

I must have heard wrong. He didn't say sperm. I've never heard an adult male say the word sperm before. I guess my previous life was more sheltered than I thought, despite having traveled all over the world.

"Um. How did they manage to take your…?" I clear my throat. "… sperm." And do I want to know?

"Sex obviously, which was surprisingly pleasurable since they can control your mind."

"But." How to put this delicately? "If you …er… ejaculated into the alien, then the sperm has been used. I'm not sure how we could get it back." I'm sure my face is flaming red considering the heat emanating from it. Am I dreaming? Surely, I'm not sitting in my office discussing sperm and ejaculation with aliens?

"They also extracted my sperm in other ways."

And I'm done. I'm not asking him how they extracted sperm. I do not want to know what 'other ways' means. There's a limit on how many times I can say sperm and ejaculate in one lifetime and I've hit it.

"I'm sorry, Mr. Havers, but I'm afraid we don't handle alien retrievals."

He frowns. "But you're the fifth investigation firm I've met with."

And I bet he's going to meet with a whole bunch more before he finds a taker.

I stand. "I'm sorry. We're a small firm. We simply don't have the manpower to pull off an operation involving aliens." Wow. I'm making stuff up as I go along, but my excuse didn't sound at all like I pulled it out of my ass. Go me.

"I understand." He stands and we shake hands.

After I escort him out of the office, I watch as he slinks along the wall of the hallway. His eyes are wide as he scans the area. I don't know what he's scanning for since there's no one around. The elevator door opens and Hailey steps out. When Mr. Havers sees her, he starts screaming before running off down the hall with his hands waving in the air.

"Don't take my sperm!" is the last thing I hear before the stairwell door shuts behind him.

Hailey shakes her head. "I take it we don't have a new client?"

"Um, no, unless you know how to retrieve sperm from aliens."

"Nope. I never did learn how to locate aliens. I could ask Wally, but I think that dude," she points her thumb in the direction of the stairs, "would shit his pants if he saw Wally."

"Probably." I agree because Wally still scares me on a good day. But if aliens do exist, he would be the one person to know about it.

We walk into the office to find Suzie bent over laughing. "And I thought the highlight of my day was going to be Lola humping you," she manages to say between bouts of laughter. "But then you have a man in here claiming to have sex with aliens. Awesome."

At her name, Lola's head pops up. Her tongue lolls out of her mouth and she stands. Oh no. I take a step back. "When is she having her little surgery?" I ask with my hands held out to hold her off. Not as if I can stop her. Lola has a mind of her own when she's feeling horny.

"The vet said we had to wait until she's six months old."

"Lola is six months old." She's actually older.

Hailey frowns. "I feel bad for her."

Lola wanders over to me and starts sniffing my leg. She stands up on her rear legs, but before she can commence humping my leg, Hailey grabs her collar and pulls her away. Needless to say, she's become an ace at cockblocking Lola. Is it still cockblocking when no cocks are involved?

Oh boy, a few months of working with Hailey and Suzie and the word cock is roaming around in my head. What words will I be able to think in a year? I can't wait to find out.

Chapter 7

THE NEXT DAY I'M trailing a cheating spouse. I mean alleged cheating spouse. I don't have the proof Mr. Kindle is a cheater – yet.

Hailey usually doesn't want me working on cheater cases as I'm too 'conspicuous'. Conspicuous? How am I conspicuous? I'm sitting in an SUV with darkened windows outside of a craptastic motel. Oh wait, that does sound a bit conspicuous.

It's not my fault Mr. Kindle likes to get his groove on with his secretary at lunch once a week at this motel. I don't get it. Why be in a committed relationship if you're going to cheat? And if you are going to cheat, why come to a place where the bedsheets most likely haven't been washed since the last visitor? Bed bugs are real, you know.

I'm not kidding about this place being crappy. It doesn't even have a name. There's simply a sign with 'Motel' on it. Of the five letters in motel, two still light up. The 'M' and the 'e' spelling

Me. How appropriate. After all, Mr. Kindle isn't thinking about anyone but himself.

I watch as a gray Cadillac pulls into the lot. What a jerk. He can afford a Cadillac, but he's not willing to splurge a little on a hotel room. Dirtbag.

I raise my camera and watch through the viewer as Mr. Kindle exits the car. He doesn't bother going around the car to open the door for his passenger. When the passenger steps out, I can't help my eye roll. Of course, his secretary is a blonde wearing a skintight dress nearly giving me a peek of her rear end. Typical. Isn't she freezing her butt off?

I snap away as the two walk to a room. Mr. Kindle produces a key from his pocket and unlocks the door. Huh. Did he already have the key? Does he keep a permanent room in this place? My nose wrinkles of its own accord. I don't want to know.

I watch as he walks in, leaving his secretary to follow. They close the door and I wait a minute before getting out of the SUV. I know I need to take pictures of them in an indelicate position, but I'm struggling with the idea of watching strangers have sex. I've never watched porn before and now I'm going to see the action live and in person.

Maybe Hailey and Suzie are right. Maybe I'm not meant to do the cheater cases. No. I refuse to believe it. This is my job. I'm not watching them have sex for fun. I'm not a voyeur. I'm a professional.

I straighten my back and march right on over to their room. The curtains are slightly open as if they couldn't be bothered to take the time to close them properly before attacking each other.

I peek inside to see both parties are naked and on the bed. Guess someone doesn't believe in foreplay. I feel for his secretary. I know what it's like to be with a man who doesn't bother to get you warmed up for the main act. It sucks. Not literally. There is no sucking involved, which is the entire problem.

I bring the camera up and snap a whole bunch of pictures. There. Done. I switch off the camera and walk back to my vehicle feeling pleased with myself. I didn't gag once. Of course, I didn't see any naked body parts besides a hairy, flabby ass. Someone needs to find a good esthetician. And maybe a personal trainer.

I walk around the front of the SUV to the driver's seat and stop dead. Shit. Damn. What is he doing here?

"Can I help you?" I pretend I don't know who he is.

"You can give me your camera," Mr. Brown demands.

I wrinkle my brow, still acting like I don't know who he is. "No." I pull the camera close to my chest. "I don't know who you are—"

He cuts me off. "Enough of the bullshit. You know exactly who I am."

I drop the act and make a demand of my own. "How did you figure out who I am?" It's not like I'm wearing a jacket advertising the firm *We Cheat, You Eat.*

He snickers. "Like it was hard."

I motion with my hand for him to continue.

"Melanie clocked your car a week ago. Got a contact who ran the plates."

Darn. It was easy to find me. Maybe we should invest in some fake license plates when we're staking out a place. Or maybe I'm not as good at being inconspicuous as I thought. I shake those thoughts right out of my head. This is not the time to worry about my job performance.

"Now. If explanation hour is done, I'll take the camera."

He holds out his hand. As if I'm going to simply hand the camera to him.

"Why do you need the camera?" I act like I'm a dumb blonde. It's not my first time pretending to be an idiot. It probably won't be my last. I thought I'd left the dumb blonde act in my past, but if it helps me out here, you won't hear me complaining.

"Don't act stupid. I need the pictures you took. Dead men can't be photographed."

What do I do now? Do I admit the pictures have already been printed and a report sent to the insurance company? His wife's claim for life insurance is going to be denied no matter whether he has my camera or not.

I shake my head. "I'm sorry. I can't help you."

"I was afraid you'd say that." He pulls a knife from behind his back. Well, shit, things went downhill fast.

I take a step back. He waves the knife around as he takes a step in my direction. "Don't move."

I am really done taking orders from men, especially men waving knives in my face. I twirl around and take off running.

There's an office on the other side of the motel. If I can reach it before Brown reaches me, I'll be safe.

Thank goodness I listened to Hailey and stopped wearing my high heels to work. I may be an expert in walking in heels, but running full out? Now is not the moment to find out.

I realize I'm huffing and puffing away but not screaming. "Help! Help!"

Screaming for help doesn't make a darn bit of difference if there's no one around. Shit. I'm going to die in the cracked parking lot of a no-name hotel. No. If I can survive my past, I can survive a swindler running at me with a knife. I'm not giving up yet. I dare a glimpse behind me. Crap. Stan Brown is gaining on me. I put on a burst of speed. Almost there.

I reach out my hand to open the door to the office, but Brown grasps my shoulder and spins me around before I can grab the door handle. He places the knife in my face and snarls at me. "Give me the camera."

I shake my head. "No."

"Then, I'll have to take it."

He reaches forward to grab the camera, and I wrap my arms around it. I refuse to give it up. After all, he can't stab me and steal my camera at the same time, can he?

"Help! Help!" I scream and use my foot to pound on the door behind me. Where is the office manager? Why isn't he out here helping me?

Tires screech and a car comes barreling into the parking lot. It slams to a halt mere feet from where Brown and I stand playing tug-a-war with my camera. A man jumps out of the car and starts running toward us.

As soon as Brown notices the man, he releases the camera and I stumble back. I fall against the office door but manage to keep my feet. Brown takes off before the man can reach us.

"Are you okay?" he asks as he looks me up and down. "Do you want me to call the police?"

"Umm…" I bite my lip. I'm not sure what I should do. "I think I'll call my boss."

"Come on. Why don't you sit in the office while you call him?"

I don't correct his assumption that my boss is a male. Now isn't the time to beat my chest and rant about women's emancipation.

He pulls out a key and my eyes widen as he unlocks the door. Holy moly. The office was locked! What would I have done if I'd known the office was locked? No, I'm not going to think about it. I'm glad I didn't know earlier.

He guides me to a fold-up chair, and I take a seat to call Hailey who calls Aiden who tells me to call the police. I guess I'm calling the police.

My hands tremble for an entirely different reason. Will the police figure out who I am? No. I refuse to believe it. My background is solid. They won't have any reason to go digging around. I hope.

Chapter 8

Do not let anyone push you around, even if they make butterflies explode in your stomach. ~ Phoebe's rules for becoming a better person

"I'm not sure why you insisted on coming with me." I frown down at Suzie. Does she think I'm too scared to go to a self-defense class alone?

"I'm your friend. I'm supporting you. It's what friends do." My heart warms at her words. I've never had real friends before. Oh, I've had tons of friends who smile to your face and then stab you in the back the minute you're looking the other direction. Those I can do without.

But then Suzie has to go and ruin the moment by opening her big fat mouth again. "Besides, check out the man candy." She wiggles her eyebrows.

I am not here to look at men. Men and their stupid games is what got me here in the first place. Stupid Stan Brown thinking it's okay to fake his death and then, when I prove him wrong, coming after me with a knife. I shudder as a tremor works its way through my body. The knife may not have touched me, but it featured prominently in my dreams last night.

"Please join us on the mats," a woman I assume is the instructor shouts.

I walk to the mat while Suzie skips along beside me. She's not looking where she's going. Of course, she isn't. Why would she start now after thirty-some years of life? She trips on the corner of the matt and goes flying. She lands on her back and jumps to her feet.

"I'm okay."

I don't bother to respond. The woman falls all the dang time. If I checked to make sure she didn't hurt herself every single time, I wouldn't have time to do anything else.

The instructor approaches Suzie. "You know how to fall. Do you mind helping me with a demonstration?"

Suzie squeals. "I'm the teacher's pet."

The instructor ignores the squeal and pulls Suzie to the middle of the mat. She claps her hands to get everyone's attention. Once everyone stops chattering away, she introduces herself, "Good evening. I'm Tabitha. I'll be your instructor for the evening."

"I'm Suzie."

"Ah, yes." Tabitha points to Suzie. "I normally don't talk about falling techniques, but since Suzie here has perfected how to fall properly," Suzie takes a bow, "I thought we'd do a quick demo."

"You want me to fall?" Suzie asks and then promptly falls forward. She doesn't stay on the ground long. She bounces to her feet and shouts "Tada!"

Tabitha takes a deep breath. I bet she's counting to ten before she slaps Suzie. I get it. I used to think I was a patient person. Then, I met Suzie. I watch as an evil gleam shines from Tabitha's eyes right before she reaches over and pushes Suzie over.

As Suzie falls, she explains, "See how she keeps her palms flat, making sure her elbows don't slam into the ground." When Suzie tries to stand, Tabitha casually places a foot on her back to keep her down. I think I like Tabitha. "She keeps her hands in front of her face to keep her head from hitting the ground."

Tabitha removes her foot and Suzie gets to her feet. She bounces on her toes. "Want me to fall again?"

Tabitha shakes her head. Suzie frowns but quickly recovers and skips over to stand next to me.

"Tonight's class is a crash course in self-defense. If anyone's interested at the end of tonight's course, I also teach in-depth courses." Tabitha paces back and forth in front of the women lined up to take the class as she lectures.

"The aim of tonight's seminar is to prepare you for how to handle an attack. We don't have time in one evening to master fighting techniques. Instead, we'll be concentrating on recognizing and avoiding dangerous situations as well as psychological preparation for an attack."

She looks around the group. "Does anyone have any questions?"

Suzie raises her arm and jumps up and down. "Me. Me. Me."

Tabitha ignores her and points to a woman on the other side of the room.

"Does self-defense work?" The woman asks.

Tabitha places her hands on her hips. "Good question. Self-defense does work. Those who take the training are less likely to experience assault and are more confident in their ability to resist assault."

Someone grabs my hand and I jump. I open my mouth to scream but a deep voice whispers in my ear, "It's me."

Me? Who's me? I look over my shoulder and notice Ryker. "What are you doing here?"

He doesn't answer. Instead, he pulls me away from the group. He leads me to the far corner of the room where he pushes me against the wall and places his hands on the wall next to my head, boxing me in. I should feel intimidated. After all, the man could snap me in two with his bare hands. I'm not, though. No, my body warms at having him near and I feel tingles in places I've never felt tingles before. Seriously, never. I didn't know you could feel tingles *there*, but I like it.

"Princess." He tucks a strand of my hair behind my ear. "Why are you here?"

And I thought I was tingling before. When he speaks in a soft voice and touches me with such gentleness, my knees go weak. The corner of his mouth kicks up in a half-smile and a dimple comes out to play. A dimple I want to lick. Oh boy. I'm sailing in unchartered waters. What do I do?

"Answer the question, Princess. Why do you need self-defense classes?"

My brain comes back online. "Because I don't want to feel helpless again."

And now I understand where the expression thunderous face comes from. If ever there was a thunderous face, I'm looking at it. "Explain."

I wave my hand to signal it's no big deal and end up smacking him in the chest. His rock hard chest. I've heard about six-pack abs but I've never seen any up close. I bet Ryker has six-pack abs. I bite my lip and my hand itches to touch.

Ryker grabs my hand and places it flat against his chest. "Explain. Now."

I clear my throat and force myself to look him in the eyes and explain about Stan Brown the dick. And if I thought Ryker's face was thunderous before, I was wrong. Because this face? If you look up thunderous in the dictionary, you'll see a picture of the face he's making right now.

I start backpedaling. "It's not a big deal. Nothing happened. But it made me aware of how dangerous my job could be. Hailey is a superhero. She can do self-defense, shoot all kinds of weapons, and disable security systems. I'm merely an unskilled woman who Hailey took a chance on."

He swears under his breath. "I should have been there."

My brow wrinkles. "Should have been there? Why? I was doing my job."

"I'm supposed to be looking out for you."

This is news to me. "You are? Why?"

"Because." He grunts as if 'because' is an answer. I don't think so.

"Look." I poke him in his chest and immediately regret it. Ouch! I shake my hand out. "Just because you're a badass bounty hunter doesn't mean I need you to look after me. I can take care of myself." At least, I'm learning how to, and I quite like it, too.

Before Ryker can respond, Suzie shouts, "Pheebs! You're missing the best part! We get to attack a man in an alien suit."

An alien suit? What is she talking about? I look over and see someone wearing one of those padded self-defense suits. He, at least I'm assuming it's a he, looks nothing like an alien.

"Do you think he'll probe me?" she shouts. The rest of the women turn to gawk at her. She raises her hands. "What?"

"I better get back there before Suzie causes a riot," I say and duck under Ryker's arm. I make it exactly one step before he grabs my t-shirt and pulls me back.

"I'm serious. I want to make sure you're safe. Protect you."

If there's a phrase likely to cause to lose my mind, it's *protect you.* I am sick and tired of people doing things to protect me when really they're saving their own skin. "Let go over my t-shirt."

He fists the shirt tighter.

"Fine." I grab the hem and whip the shirt off. No biggie. I've worn bikini tops that show more skin than the sports bra I'm wearing.

Ryker's eyes widen as he takes a step back. "This isn't over," he declares before throwing my shirt at me.

I catch my shirt and roll my eyes. "Whatever." I stomp away from him. I do not need a man to come butting into my life and telling me what to do. I've had enough of those kinds of men for the rest of my life, thank you very much.

Chapter 9

For every action, there is an equal and opposite prank. ~ Phoebe's rules for becoming a better person

I NEARLY RUN INTO Hailey and Suzie when they stop right inside the entrance of McGraw's Pub as I'm following them into the bar the next night.

"What's up?" I ask as I peek around them. My eyes widen when I see the place is packed. 'Packed' as in wall-to-wall people with every table taken, and a crowd three-deep at the bar.

"Hailey!" Sid shouts and waves at us from their table.

Once we reach them, Hailey wastes no time attacking. "What did you do?"

Wally is the picture of innocence. "Us? Why do you think we did anything?"

Hailey snorts and crosses her arms over her chest.

Suzie claps and squeals. "How fun! Is it like a dating thing? You're the only men here, so I guess we get to pick out women for you."

Sid, the old dog, grins as does Barney. Wally and Lenny, though, look like they want to strangle Suzie and bury her somewhere no one will find her. I know the feeling, although I have no idea how to hide a body. I'm pretty sure Wally and Lenny do, though.

"Maybe you shouldn't antagonize the men who can break you in two with a flick of a finger."

Suzie laughs. "Please. The uncles would never hurt me." She bats her eyelashes. "Would you?"

"Define hurt," Wally demands.

Suzie leans forward and plants her hands on the table. She isn't looking at what she's doing. Why would she start now? The beer mugs on the table shake and a coffee cup falls over.

"Suzie the menace," Barney mutters. "Which reminds me … What do you call a nanny with breast implants?" He looks around but no one answers him. "A faux-pair."

"Stop trying to distract me. What did you do?" Hailey is not playing around. She is m-a-d. Mad.

The uncles all pretend to be super interested in their beer bottles.

"I got this," Suzie says and taps the woman in a chair at the table behind her on the shoulder. "Hi! What are you doing here?"

"What am I doing here?" The woman looks Suzie up and down. "What are you doing here is the question. You don't have a chance with the silver fox."

At the words 'silver fox', Hailey growls. Her pops is a total silver fox. He may be twenty-some years my senior, but I would totally take him for a ride. Assuming I was up for taking rides with any man. But I am not interested in men. No matter how weak my knees go when Ryker touches me.

Hailey approaches the woman. "Why do *you* think you have a chance with the silver fox?"

"Duh." The woman pulls out her phone. "It says right here he's lonely and looking for someone to warm his bed at night."

Hailey nabs the phone from the woman. She protests but Hailey holds up her hand to silence her. "Since when does McGraw's Pub have a twitter account? And why is Pops' picture the background image?"

I look over her shoulder and sure enough, Pops is smiling back at me from the McGraw's Pub twitter page. The account has only tweeted once and it's a doozy.

Please join me at McGraw's for two for one drinks at happy hour. PS I'm lonely and looking for a woman who can keep my bed warm at night.

"What the hell? We don't have two for one drinks at happy hour." Hailey glares at the uncles. Personally, I would have been more concerned about them pimping out my dad but whatever.

"Can I have my phone back now?"

Hailey practically throws the thing at the stranger before stomping to the bar. "Good thing I didn't bring Lola with me tonight."

"Good. She's gone. Now, you can tell me what Pops did." Suzie scoots into the booth while Sid stands to find a chair for me to sit on.

"He put salt in my coffee," Wally admits.

"Salt in your coffee? This seems a bit of an over the top response for salt in your coffee."

Suzie's one to talk. She has a college degree in over the top responses. "Because you've never overreacted."

She ignores me and points to Wally. "Explain."

"Have you ever had a rough night where you barely got any sleep? The one thing you know is going to get you through the day is a cup of coffee. You can practically taste the caffeine goodness. But then when you take a sip, it's undrinkable because someone put salt in it."

"Okay. When you put it like that." Suzie easily gives in. "But Pops is going to get you back after this. I'd sleep with one eye open if I were you."

"Wally always sleeps with one eye open," Lenny says. I can believe it. The man is on high alert all the time. It doesn't matter that we're sitting in a bar having a drink and not on some mountaintop on the lookout for rebel soldiers.

"Here." Pops sets a martini down in front of me and a Guinness in front of Suzie. "The rest of you fuckers can wait in line at the bar."

"Good to see you, darling." He kisses my hair and warmness fills my body. No one, absolutely no one, has ever been happy to see me. And no one has kissed my hair and made me feel welcome *and* part of the family.

"Will you adopt me?" The words pop out before I can stop them.

I expect everyone to chuckle at my faux-pax. Instead, their gazes zero in on me like they're trying to read my thoughts. Oh god. Please don't tell me the military has perfected mind-reading.

"Where's your family, darling?" Pops asks.

I look him directly in the eyes and straight-up lie. "I don't have one." Not one I claim at least.

"Pops!" Hailey shouts from behind the bar. Phew. Saved by the bell.

Pops squeezes my shoulder before sauntering off. I watch him leave and release the breath I was holding. I look up to find the uncles are still studying me. Guess I'm not saved by the bell after all.

"Where did you grow up, Phoebe?"

"Is Adams your real last name?"

"Have you been married before?"

"Are you an orphan?"

"Did you grow up in care?"

I'm bombarded with question after question. Even if I wanted to keep up, I couldn't at this point. If there's such a thing as attack by question, this is it.

"Nope. Stop. You're making her uncomfortable." My mouth falls open at Suzie's words. Considering how much the woman has been bugging me to tell her my life story since we met, I didn't expect her to be in my corner.

Suzie winks at me. "I got your back."

"Moving on then. How are you doing after the knife incident?" Lenny asks.

"Knife incident?" I pretend I have no idea what he's talking about.

"Don't play innocent with us, Doll. We can sniff a lie from a mile away."

"But how do—" I stop when I notice Suzie squirming in her seat. So much for having my back. Someone is a blabbermouth.

"Come on." She shrugs. "It's the most exciting thing to happen this month. Well, except for the guy who thinks aliens stole his sperm. Talk about hilarious."

"Dead serious now, Doll. How are you doing?" I can tell by the look on Lenny's face he is not letting me get away with evading the question, but I'm not about to tell him I've been having nightmares of a giant rottweiler chasing me with a knife. And yes, I realize dogs do not have opposable thumbs and would never be able to hold a knife.

"I'm okay. The self-defense class helped."

"Sure. It helped you. I didn't get anything out of it," Suzie complains.

"If you would have stopped calling the guy in the protection suit an alien and saying you wanted to have sex with him, she wouldn't have kicked you out of the class."

Suzie is the only person I know who could get herself kicked out of a free community center class for women by being inappropriate. I'm sure she thought she was being funny, but it's not funny to joke about sex at a self-defense class full of women who want to protect themselves from sexual assault.

"What? Mr. Havers got me to thinking. What if there are aliens? Would the sex with them be good?"

Barney leans forward. "Who is Mr. Havers? Was he an alien?"

I need a break from the aliens. Suzie hasn't shut up about it since the Havers visit. I'm off to the restroom despite not needing the facilities. After I re-do my make-up and wash my hands, I check my phone. There's a message from an unknown number.

I'm off to chase a skip. Make sure to let the vets watch out for you

Huh? *Who is this?*

Ryker

Why is Ryker texting me? And how did he get my number? And who does he think he is?

I can take care of myself

I send the message and switch off my phone. First, he barges in on my self-defense class and now he steals my phone number and orders me around. I don't care how many tingles I get when the man touches me. I am done with men who order me around.

When I exit the woman's restroom, Wally is waiting on me. Of course, he is.

"What's up, Wally?" I pretend to be clueless and bat my eyelashes for good measure.

He tags me around my neck and pulls me close. "There's no need to be brave in front of us. We're here if you need us." He waits on my nod before continuing. "Anything you need, kid. All you have to do is ask."

My eyes sting and I have to blink fast before tears fall. I have never had anyone I could rely on before. It's almost too good to be true. Please be true.

Chapter 10

It's not stalking when you know the person in real life. ~ Phoebe's rules for becoming a better person

OF ALL THE CRAZY things I've done, this ranks as one of the craziest. Maybe *the* craziest. Following a former soldier who I'm pretty sure is still involved with the government is some Black Ops type of situation. Worse yet, this is not the first time I've followed Wally the super-soldier. No, I've followed him a few times now. Am I stalker? No, I know him. It's not stalking when you know the guy, right?

I watch as Wally parks his Dodge Charger in the driveway of a ranch house. I study the gray building as he disappears into it. If I had to guess the kind of place he lived in, ranch house wouldn't even make the list. I assumed he lived in some glass high-rise downtown. I guess I don't know him as well as I thought. The sneaky man likes to keep things close to his chest.

And just why am I following Wally? A man who has been nothing but kind to me? Well, I'm in a tight spot – the tightest of tight stops. I'm nearly out of money and my rent is due soon. Despite living in an absolute pit, I don't have the cash for rent.

It is no joke to call my place a pit. I rent a room above a dentist's office downtown. And by room, I do mean a single room. I have to share a bathroom and kitchen with the other renters. The other renters are the kind of people I usually cross the street to avoid. Case in point? One of the guys on my floor has a teardrop tattoo. I have no idea if the tattoo means he killed someone or if that's an urban myth, but I'd definitely cross the street if I saw him coming just in case.

And don't get me started on all the food they've stolen from me. I sold my Prada tote to buy a small refrigerator and hot plate for my room. I'm running out of things to sell, though. My BMW was the first to go. I managed to live nearly a year on the money until I realized I needed to find a job.

But since I couldn't tell anyone about my college degree – I'm not sure how a degree in social anthropology would help me anyway – and I had absolutely no job experience, I wasn't exactly swamped in job offers. All the waitressing jobs wanted someone with experience and practically every other job required a background check. I took a chance when I saw the ad for help by *You Cheat, We Eat*. I can't believe they offered me a job.

I'm still not a licensed PI, though, which means I don't get a regular paycheck. I've had to sell most of my designer clothes to have enough money to live on. The clothes may have been worth a bundle when I bought them, but the re-sale value leaves a lot to be desired. Good thing the PI uniform of jeans, t-shirt, and sweater is much cheaper.

The door to the SUV opens and I whirl around with my hand raised. Before I get a chance to flail about, Wally grabs my raised hand and pulls me out of the vehicle. He nabs the key from the ignition before marching me into the house.

My eyes widen as I take in the interior of his ranch house. This is not the suburban house the exterior leads you to expect it is. Not at all. The floors are hardwood, the walls are painted an eggshell white, and the furniture is sleek, modern leather. The kitchen is more of the same with its marble countertops and gray, shiny cabinets.

I need to stop judging things by their appearances. I should know better. Look at me. I'm wearing Fendi boots, Michael Kors jeans, and a cashmere Louis Vuitton sweater. One glance at me and people think I have money to burn. Not anymore, I don't. Sure, I used to have money, but I'm currently standing in a man's house who is practically a stranger to me to beg him for cash.

Oh god, this was a bad idea. I pivot on my heel to leave. I can't do this. Wally stops me. "Sit."

I drop my butt on the leather couch. His voice does not broker a discussion. He marches to the kitchen, opens the refrigerator, and pulls out two water bottles. He returns to the living area and throws a water bottle at me before taking a seat on the couch opposite me.

"How did you find me?"

"I followed you." It wasn't hard.

"You? You followed me?"

"Yeah, me." Now, I'm starting to feel offended. It's not like I don't know how to follow someone. It's not rocket science. Besides, there are a ton of YouTube guides you can watch.

"Explain."

I wrinkle my nose as I stare at him. I don't know how better to explain it than I followed his car from A to B. Oh wait. I didn't follow from A to B. I followed from A to C and then from C to B. It sounds confusing but it's really not.

"I followed you two days ago from McGraw's until you hit East Locust." At which point, I looked around and realized we were the only two cars on the road. If I had continued to follow him, he'd have made me for sure. I wasn't sure I wanted him to see me. At least not yet. "Then yesterday, I waited at East Locust until I saw your Charger drive by."

"Damn, kid. Maybe you've got what it takes for this investigator business after all."

My smile stretches from ear to ear at his compliment.

"Too bad your situational awareness is crap." The smile falls from my face. "Otherwise, I wouldn't have scared you when I opened the door."

Oh yeah. I deflate. I do need to work on being aware of my surroundings. Brown got the drop on me as well. Tabitha did say situational awareness is the first step in self-defense. Maybe I should sign up for her advanced class. Yeah, right. Broke, remember?

"What are you doing here?"

I bite my lip as I pretend to find the floor fascinating. I was still mulling over my decision to bother him when he hauled me out of the SUV. Do I really want to lay myself bare to him?

"I'm not mad, Phoebe. But you obviously went to a lot of trouble to get me alone. I assume you have a good reason."

I feel a twist in my wrist, and I realize I'm wringing my hands. I pull my hands apart and set them on my thighs. Showing nervousness is never a good idea, whether in this life or my previous one.

"I … um… could use some help."

Wally goes on high alert. "Are you in danger?"

I wave his question away. "No, I'm not in danger." I escaped my old life. I was initially worried they'd come after me, but it's been more than a year, and no one has come sniffing around. I'm in the clear. But I'm not waving any red capes at the bull.

I take a deep breath and dive in. "What I am is broke."

"Kid, I'm a man and even I can tell those clothes are worth a shit ton of money."

"Yeah, well, I took these from my old life. I've sold most of the clothes now."

"You sold your clothes?"

I look up to see he's frowning and tilting his head as he studies me.

"It's not like I have access to any other money." I threw away all my credit cards and bank cards before I left. I didn't need to be a PI to know how easy electronic transfers are to follow.

To his credit, Wally doesn't question me further. "What do you need?"

Those words are why I'm here. When he said he'd do any-thing I need, an idea sparked in my head. "I need two things actually, but you can't tell anyone."

He grunts. "Depends on the two things."

I stand. I'm not going to tell him I need to pass a background check unless he promises to keep quiet. I don't want or need anyone up in my business.

"Sit!" he barks, and my body follows his order before my mind realizes he spoke.

"Let's try this again. I will keep your secrets." I smile. "But…" Ugh. There's always a but. "If you are in any danger, then the deal's off."

"I'm not in danger," I rush to say. I'm not lying. My past life is in my past. They're probably as happy to be rid of me as I am of them.

"Okay. What do you need?"

"Can I have a loan? I don't have enough money to pay rent this month."

His brow wrinkles. "Aren't you earning money working with Hailey?"

This leads me to favor number two. "Until I'm a licensed PI, I'm working as an unpaid intern. She pays me off the books for some stuff, but …" I trail off with a shrug.

"Why aren't you licensed? You're a smart gal. I'm sure you can pass the test in one go."

"I haven't taken the exam yet. I haven't been able to apply for my license yet."

"Why not?"

"There's a little problem with the federal background check."

Wally bends forward. "Are you a felon, Phoebe?"

I shake my head. I've never committed a crime in my life. Buying a fake ID when you're an adult isn't a crime, is it? "No. But I can't pass a background check."

He leans back and drums his fingers against his thigh. "Does this have anything to do with Phoebe Adams only existing since last year?"

I nod. I'm such an idiot. I paid a ton of money for a new identity. I didn't realize I needed to specifically ask for a background for my entire life. To me it was obvious. I didn't know there was a problem until Suzie started bugging me about my missing background. The woman thinks I'm in witness protection. The woman does not pass go; she heads straight to nutsville.

"And you want me to what? Make sure you can pass a federal background check?"

I bite my lip. "Can you?" If there's anyone who can provide me with a background, it's Wally.

He's quiet for a while, long enough for me to get nervous. Will he tell Hailey what I asked? Will she fire me? What am I going to do for money if I don't have a job?

"Here's the deal. I will give you some money to tide you over."

"I'll pay you back. I promise."

He holds up his hand. "This is not a loan. This is me investing in your future." When I open my mouth to protest, he shakes his hand. "No, Phoebe. These are my terms. Take it or leave it."

I nod. I can hardly leave it.

"And I will ensure you pass your background check." I release the breath I was holding. Thank goodness. "But if I think you are in any danger, then I will not only tell the others, but I will not hesitate to step in and take care of things."

"I'm not in danger," I insist.

"And I need to know your real name."

My eyes widen. "Why?"

"Kid, I'm not making sure you can pass a background check without checking your real background."

Darn. He has a point. "It's Abbot."

"Thank you."

"Why are you thanking me? I'm the one who's thankful." Hailey's uncles are confusing.

"Thank you for trusting me." He stands. "Now, wait here. I'll get you some cash."

I watch as he strolls out of the room. I can't believe he's going to help me. And he's going to keep my secret. *It's okay, Phoebe. Everything is going to be okay.*

Chapter 11

Flirting is a necessary skill in every woman's
arsenal regardless of whether she's a 'lady' or not.
~ Phoebe's rules for becoming a better person

"How is your tall, dark, dangerous looking drink of water?" Hailey asks with a wiggle of her brows.

I play stupid. "You mean Ryker?"

She rolls her eyes. "No, Wally." She snort laughs, but my heart stops. Does she know I went to Wally? Did he tell everyone my real name? What was I thinking? I can't trust anyone. I should know better!

Hailey hip checks me. "Come on. I want all the details about Ryker."

My breath rushes out of me. She's joking. She doesn't know about my deal with Wally. "You sound like Suzie," I say to buy myself some time.

I don't have any gossip to share with her. Seriously. I've seen the guy a few times, but it's not like we're dating. I don't even have his phone number. Well, I guess I do. Assuming the number he texted me from is his number. But his bossing me around by text did not fill my stomach with butterflies. Not like when he came up to me before he left the self-defense class and whispered in my ear, "See you around, Princess." The memory of his gravely voice whispering in my ear gives me goosebumps.

"Fine. Keep your secrets," Hailey grumps but then she winks. "What must people think when they see us together?"

My head can't keep up with the change in topic. "What do you mean?"

"You looking like sex on a stick. And then there's me." She indicates herself with a sweep of her arm up and down her body.

I roll my eyes. She has no idea how beautiful a woman she is. Sure, she's dressed in ripped jeans, boots, and a leather jacket that has seen better days, but she owns the look. I'd kill for a mere drop of her confidence.

As opposed to Hailey's casual look, I'm dressed like a man-eater. On purpose, mind you. I'm not literally a man-eater. I subsist on a diet of vegetables and rice for gosh sakes. Men are not on my list of approved foods.

And why am I dressed like a woman of questionable virtue? We're setting up one of our honeypot traps tonight. This is the original reason I was hired by *We Cheat, You Eat.* To ambush men who are stepping out on their wives.

When a wife has doubts about the ability of her husband to keep it in his pants, we step in. Don't get me wrong. I don't do anything with the men beyond a bit of not-so-harmless-flirting. But I do need to dress the part. Thus, why I'm wearing a Furstenberg wrap dress with my Louboutin heels.

This is why I haven't sold all of the clothes from my previous life. I could most likely fetch a pretty penny for both items, but I need something sexy to wear for these adventures in flirting.

"What's the setup for tonight?" I ask although the setup is almost always the same.

"Mrs. Jackson thinks her husband is cheating on her. She has no proof." They never do. "But she's about had it with him coming home drunk on Wednesday nights after she's wrestled the kids into bed all by herself."

"Drunk and smelling like perfume?"

She shakes her head. "No. I asked. No perfume smells or lipstick stains but the drinking occurs at the bar of the Grand Hotel…" She trails off with a shrug. She need say no more. There's a reason all of our honeypot traps are set at this hotel. Apparently, adulterers aren't very creative when it comes to picking out hotels to cheat in.

"What's the husband's name?"

"Albert."

"How old is he?" Because Albert sounds like a grandfather, not a carouser.

"I didn't ask, but Mrs. Jackson is middle-aged. If I had to guess, I'd say late thirties."

She hands me a picture of the couple. Albert is staring down at his wife with a smile on his face while she gazes up at him like he's her entire world. The couple look happy and in love. I hope he isn't cheating on her and throwing her love away.

We walk into the Grand Hotel and Peggy, the receptionist, waves at us with a huge smile on her face. Peggy is a twenty-something who thinks the honeypot schemes are hilarious. Personally, I don't think there's a single thing funny about men who cheat.

Hailey veers off to get a room key from Peggy while I head to the bar. My butt barely has a chance to hit a barstool before Andy, the bartender, sets a martini in front of me.

"Phoebe, it's been a while," he says as he looks me up and down. Men. They're all the same. Show a little bit of cleavage and they start panting like dogs in heat. Hold up. That doesn't make sense. Boy dogs don't go into heat. Anyway, you get what I'm saying.

I take a sip of my martini and moan in delight. Normally, Andy waters down my drink down to the point you could probably serve it to a toddler. It's Hailey's rule. She thinks I'm going to get drunk and belligerent. The joke's on her. I've never been belligerent a day in my life. But who knows? Maybe the new Phoebe has belligerent in her?

Hailey glides by and leaves a keycard on the bar in front of me. She acts like we don't know each other. I barely hold in my eye roll. I'm not sure who she's afraid is going to see us together. No one's here yet. We always arrive at least fifteen minutes early, and the bar is no-man's-land until the businesses in the area close for the day.

Andy places his elbows on the bar and leans toward me. "How have you been, sweet thing?"

Sweet thing? I am not here to flirt with Andy. It's bad enough I have to flirt with some guy I've never met before. Don't get me wrong, I am an expert at flirting. If you could get a degree in it, I'd have a doctorate by now. But it's not like I enjoy it. No, flirting was a survival skill in my previous life.

I hear laughter right before a group of men enter the bar. Andy straightens and walks to the other side of the bar to do his job. Good. One less uncomfortable conversation I need to have.

I swivel on my barstool to ensure the group of men get a good look at my cleavage. Yes, I realize I'm a hypocrite. I was ready to tear Andy's head off for looking and now I'm practically daring men to look. Total hypocrite.

I search the crowd of men and recognize Albert at the back of the group. He's laughing with the other men and not paying one bit of attention to me. Time to dial up the heat. I lean forward slightly and cross my legs. Several of the men in the group come to a stop as their eyes zero in on my legs. Gotcha!

I flutter my lashes and sway my foot. While some of the men walk to the bar to order, another group splits off and heads in my direction. Damn it. Albert is not among the group approaching.

"Buy you a drink?"

I glance at the man from under my lashes and bite my lip. I don't want him buying me a drink. Albert needs to buy me a drink. Otherwise, this night is a waste.

"Um… what about him?" I point to Albert. "He's yummy."

The man chuckles. "Good luck there. Al is devoted to his wife."

Well, shit. Is he serious? My phone beeps and by the sound, I know it's Hailey. "Excuse me."

Wrong guy. Get rid of him.

Duh. I'm not blind. I know it's the wrong guy.

He says Albert is faithful

While I'm typing, the man saunters off and joins his group. Once everyone in the group has a drink, they move to a table in the back of the bar. Huh. This has never happened before. I stand, intent on approaching Hailey and asking her what I should do, but I run smackdab into a brick wall.

"Excuse me," I say without looking up. The brick wall doesn't move, forcing me to look at who it is. "Ryker? What are you doing here?"

"Stopping you from making a fool of yourself."

"A fool of myself?" I try to walk around him, but he moves to block me. "I'm working."

"And you're going to crash and burn. Your target is not a cheater."

"How do you know?" I hold up my hand to stop his reply. I don't want to hear it. "How did you know I'd be here?"

"Babe," he grunts.

"Ugh! Babe is not an answer." I have the strangest inclination to stomp my foot. I've never stomped my foot in my life. I've stomped around, sure. But stomped my foot like a commoner? Never.

"Did you forget I'm a bounty hunter?"

No, I didn't, but I have done some research in the meantime. "Bounty hunters are illegal in Wisconsin."

"Never said I was from Wisconsin."

I don't have time for this. "I need to get back to work." Wally may have given me some money to tide me over yesterday, but I'm counting on the cash from tonight's work to help me through the next month. Christmas is not cheap.

"There's nothing for you to do. He's not going to fall for your trap. No matter how gorgeous the trap is."

He looks me up and down and his eyes heat. My belly warms and my body tingles at the look. I take a step back. Tingles are bad. I don't need any distractions right now.

"Regardless, I have a job to do." I am not going to be pushed around by a man – or anyone – ever again. My body may want to melt into his arms, but it's not happening. Nope. No melting will be occurring.

Ryker leans over and gets all in my face. "I don't think so."

I raise an eyebrow and straighten my backbone. "You don't think so? I hate to break it to you, but your opinion does not matter in this instance."

"You good, Phoebe?" Hailey asks from next to Ryker.

"Ryker was just leaving."

"I am not leaving."

"Yeah, bud, you are," Andy says. He's several inches shorter than Ryker, but he isn't backing down. "Do you want me to call security?"

Ryker glares at Andy for a long moment and I hold my breath. I do not want men fighting over me. I am not *that* woman. I'm about to pass out from lack of air when Ryker grunts and strolls off without another word. I watch him leave, but he doesn't look back. Is he gone for good? My heart squeezes at the thought.

Chapter 12

Opportunities don't always knock. Sometimes they shove their way into your room. ~ Phoebe's rules for becoming a better person

I GROAN AT THE knock on my door in the boarding house. The last time I opened the door when someone knocked, the guy standing there did not smell flowery fresh. He wanted to know if I had any ice. I told him to go look in the freezer. He came back two minutes later pissed he couldn't find what he was looking for. I Googled ice and haven't opened my door since.

"Open up, Princess. I know you're in there."

What the heck? Why is Ryker here? Well, I'm not going to find out. I do not want to talk to him after he went all caveman on me yesterday. I don't care how much my body wants to take his for a test drive. It's not happening.

"You've got thirty seconds before I open the door."

Open my door? Who does he think he is? I stomp to the door and yank it open.

"How did you know where I lived?" He opens his mouth and I cut him off. "And if you grunt babe, I'll kick you in your nuts." I won't. I've never kicked anyone in my life. Let alone in the nuts.

Hell, I've never threatened to kick someone in his nuts before. I gotta admit I'm liking the new Phoebe. She's kind of feisty.

Instead of scowling at me, Ryker smirks. "I'm a bounty hunter. Finding people is what I do."

"How did you get inside the building?"

There's supposed to be a locked door to ensure the riffraff from the street doesn't gain entrance into the building. Never mind most of the residents are riffraff. But, unfortunately, most of the residents leave the door open because they're constantly losing their keys. Apparently, it's hard to keep track of your keys when you're off your face.

Ryker looks left and right in the hallway before placing his hand on my stomach and pushing me into the room. He shuts the door behind him and then crosses his arms over his chest before staring me down. His biceps pop and I have to restrain my hands from reaching out to touch them. How do rock hard muscles feel to touch?

"Why are you living here?"

"I asked my question first." Apparently, new Phoebe is also stubborn. Good for her.

He grunts. "Outside door was unlocked."

This is getting ridiculous. I need to talk to the landlord about that door.

Ryker places his hand under my chin and lifts my head. "Why are you living here, Princess?"

"What does it matter to you?"

His hand on my chin flexes. "It matters."

"Ugh. It's all I can afford. There. Are you happy now?"

He growls. "No, I most certainly am not happy."

Whatever. It's not his problem. "What are you doing here?"

He clears his throat and steps back to remove a package from the pocket of his leather jacket. "I came to apologize for my behavior yesterday."

My jaw drops to the floor. To. The. Floor. No one – and I do mean absolutely no one – has apologized to me before. Not in my entire life. Let alone given me a present as an apology.

"Here." He shoves the package at me.

I grab it and forget all the ladylike rules my mother tried to embed in my brain and rip the wrapping off. "A pair of gloves? You bought me a pair of gloves?"

"These are smartphone gloves, but I figure they'll work with cameras, too."

"Smartphone gloves?"

"Yeah. You can operate your screen while wearing them. These also have gripper dots on the palms for a better grip." I'm speechless as I study the gift. "I'm sorry. I know you're used to better, but I thought—"

"Shut up!" I shout and then launch myself at him. "Thank you. Thank you." I peck kisses over his face and then step back to try on the gloves. They're soft and, despite not being bulky, feel warm.

"You ready?"

Is Ryker the most confusing man in the world or what? "Ready for what?"

"The second half of my apology."

I giggle. "There's no need. The gloves are perfect."

I've had my eye on a pair of Ralph Lauren wool touch gloves, but they are way out of my price range. I need to learn how to shop in my price range, but since my prince range is currently free, I'm thinking I need to stop window shopping and feeling sorry for myself when I can't afford anything.

"Get your coat."

"Do not boss me around."

He ignores my order as his eyes sweep my room. It isn't much, but I did the best with what I have. I bought one of those contraptions for dorm rooms with a raised bed and a couch underneath for my 'living room'. In the opposite corner is a small area designated as my 'kitchen'. It's not much – a desk with my hot plate on it and a shelf above it with some plates. There's also a refrigerator under the desk. Next to my 'kitchen' is a small table pushed against the wall with a single stool.

Ryker walks forward and snatches my coat from the coat rack. "It's cold out. Bundle up."

I open my mouth to argue with him but then my stomach grumbles.

"I'm buying." Those are the magic words. I put on my coat and motion for him to proceed me out of the door.

The minute I step outside, the wind whips in my face, and I shiver. This is my first winter living up north and I am freezing. Suzie warned me I haven't seen anything yet. Something not to look forward to. Ryker puts his arm around me and ushers me to his truck.

"Where are we going?" I ask once we're in his truck and pulling away from the curb.

"Somewhere I can feed you."

You won't hear any arguments from me.

We drive ten minutes and pull up to a bar and grille. "Why don't we go to McGraw's if we're going to a pub anyway?"

"Maybe I want you alone," he says before jumping out of the truck.

Before I can open my door, he's there helping me out. He grabs my hand and leads me into the bar. The bar isn't much different than McGraw's except there are several dartboards in one corner. The rest is the same – green upholstery, shiny bar with a variety of different whiskeys displayed, and pool tables in a far corner.

We grab a table and start the process of pulling off all our winter gear. Another thing I'm not liking about the northern climate. I look like a giant Pillsbury doughboy when I'm all bundled up. And while the doughboy pulls off cute without a hitch, I most certainly don't. Being fashionable when it's freezing out is impossible, although why I care about being fashionable any more is beyond me.

The waitress approaches and Ryker orders without looking at the menu. "We'll have two hamburgers and two beers." Once she nods and leaves, he explains, "They don't have your vodka here."

I roll my eyes. I don't exactly own the Stolichnaya distillery.

"And don't start up about wanting to eat rabbit foot. You've lost too much weight as it is."

What? How does he know I've lost weight? I mean, I have but not on purpose. When you're living on limited funds, rent gets paid before groceries. Now, there's a lesson I never thought I would have to learn. I've never been on a budget in my life. Not when I was fifteen and going to the mall with my friends and not when I was a college student.

To be honest, I have no interest in rabbit food right now. Rabbit food does nothing to fill my empty stomach. You'd think I'd be used to being hungry, having dieted my entire life to make sure I fit into an 'appropriate' size for a lady. But there is a huge difference between eating fresh fruit and vegetables while dieting and not having any food to eat at all. Huge.

"Where are you from?" I ask while we wait for our food.

He raises an eyebrow and I'm convinced he's not going to answer my question but then he says, "California."

My hands tremble and I place them in my lap to hide my reaction. I do not want to think about California. Moving on. "How long did you think you'll be in Wisconsin?"

He shrugs. "As long as it takes."

"As long as what takes?" The man talks in riddles.

"Babe." I know what his grunt means. It means he won't be answering my question. And I thought Wally was a man of mystery.

Our beers and burgers arrive. My eyes practically bulge out of my head at the size of the burger. And there is a mound – seriously, a mound – of fries on my plate. I've never eaten this much fatty food in my life, let alone at one sitting. But no one's stopping me with her little shakes of her head and downturned nose from digging in now.

"Tell me about yourself," Ryker asks as he picks up his burger.

The question throws me. It's definitely a date question. Is this a date? Or is it an apology dinner? I've never been on an apology dinner, but I've been on plenty of dates. I look around the cozy pub where everyone is dressed in jeans and boots. This doesn't feel like a date. Guess it's an apology dinner. And no, I'm not disappointed. At least that's what I'm telling myself.

After we eat, we play a few rounds of darts. Try to play in my case. I couldn't hit the target if it were as big as the side of a barn. I finally give up, and Ryker takes me home. He escorts me to my door and kisses my forehead. "Lock up," he orders as he steps back.

Kiss on the forehead? Totally not a date. And why does that thought cause a pit of disappointment to develop in my stomach? *You've sworn off men, Phoebe. Remember?*

Chapter 13

If you can't bake, fake it with a store-bought cake.
~ Phoebe's rules for becoming a better person

It's Thanksgiving and the grocery store is packed. I've never been to a grocery store on a holiday before. Every single person in here looks stressed out. To be honest, I'm one of those stressed out beings. I can't show up at Thanksgiving empty-handed, but what do I bring?

I was shocked when Hailey invited me to Thanksgiving with her family. She's my boss and friend – dare I say good friend? – but holidays are for family. At least that's what all the books I've read and movies I've watched claim. In real life, I have no idea what family gatherings are like first-hand. In Phoebe's previous life, holidays were all about cultivating business relationships and schmoozing new connections. The children were relegated to the care of the nanny.

Why am I thinking about my past life? It's done. Over with.

Anyway, Pops has a Thanksgiving meal in the early afternoon with the family including all the uncles. Then, he opens the pub for people who have nowhere to go on the holiday. He's such a sweetheart. I wish he were my dad.

Enough lollygagging. I need to find something to bring with me. I thought about flowers. But bringing flowers to a pub? Not the best idea. But cake's a good idea, right? Everyone loves cake, don't they? If not, more for me.

I stare at the endless number of cakes in the long ass aisle in the grocery store with no idea what to buy. I've never bought a cake in a grocery store before. To be honest, I've never bought a cake period. If I wanted a cake in my previous life, I had the cook make one. But old Phoebe is no more. New Phoebe doesn't have a cook and has exactly twenty dollars to spend if she skips lunch for the next week. Screw it. I grab the cake closest to twenty dollars. Done.

Chaos reigns when I open the door to McGraw's Pub thirty minutes later. The uncles are moving the tables, while Suzie bounces around directing them. They ignore her. As they should. Pops is yelling at the turkey in the kitchen, and Hailey and Aiden are making out in one of the booths.

I stand in the entryway for a few minutes before Suzie notices me and skips over. "What did you bring?" She grabs the cake before I have a chance to tell her. "Oh, chocolate fudge cake with chocolate frosting. Good choice." She runs off with my cake. I dash after her.

"Dessert is served!" she shouts as she enters the kitchen where a tornado appears to have touched down. I've never been in here before, but I can't imagine, the usual cook, Carol leaves it such a mess.

"Um… do you need help?" Although he's taking his own life in his hands if he asks me to help cook.

"Darling." Pops sets down the spoon he was using to stir a pot on the stove and comes over to kiss my cheek. "Happy Thanksgiving."

I beam up at him. "Happy Thanksgiving. I brought a cake." Oh shoot. Do you announce your gift? Did I make another faux pas?

"Thanks, darling. Now, get out there, grab a drink, and go enjoy yourself."

My eyes rove around the kitchen once more. "You sure you don't need help?"

He doesn't bother to respond and walks back to the stove. I guess that's a no then.

I walk back into the pub to see the uncles have moved all the tables to create one long table, which Hailey and Suzie are setting. When Suzie sees me, she drops the bundle of silverware in her hand and skips to me. Does she not realize skipping is for children? Not grown women? I shake my head to evict my mother's voice. Darn woman doesn't pay rent, she needs to leave.

"Where's Ryker?"

I'm confused. "What do you mean where's Ryker?"

"You didn't invite him?"

"Was I supposed to?"

Suzie rolls her eyes. "Duh. You always invite the boyfriend to Thanksgiving. Don't you know anything about celebrating holidays?"

Actually, no, but she doesn't need any more clues about my past. She's way too curious about it as is. My past life is part of ancient history. Nothing she needs to know about. And, anyway, Ryker isn't my boyfriend. We've been on exactly one non-date. I may be inexperienced in relationships, but I know one non-date does not a boyfriend make.

Before she can quiz me further, Pops walks out of the kitchen carrying a huge turkey. My eyes widen. How many people is he expecting?

"He makes turkey sandwiches from the leftovers for the pub tonight," Hailey answers my unasked question.

We gather around the table as Pops brings dish after dish out of the kitchen. There's mashed potatoes, green beans, cranberry sauce, and a whole bunch of other stuff I've never seen before. It smells and looks delicious. My stomach rumbles and I may be drooling.

My previous Thanksgiving meals were always catered affairs with tiny bites you could eat while standing up. I usually ended up raiding the kitchen for a sandwich, which drove my mother to distraction. A lady does not spend time in the kitchen. Why not? *Because* was always her answer. As if 'because' alone can be an answer. I'm done with her rules, I remind myself.

Once we're settled, the food starts circulating and everyone digs in. The uncles are sitting on one side of the table, while the rest of us sit across from them. Barney has a smirk on his face, and he keeps sending furtive glances toward Pops. I'd ask what he's up to, but I'm afraid of the answer.

Someone lets off a stream of gas. I keep eating and pretend I didn't hear. Mother always taught me to ignore bodily functions and noises. On this, I agree with her. No sense embarrassing someone over something they can't help.

The noises get louder. The uncles are chuckling and staring at Pops who is fidgeting and shifting from side to side in his chair. Poor guy must not be feeling well. I'm wondering if I should offer him a Tums when his phone rings.

He grabs it from his back pocket and starts cussing. "You fuckers! A fart app? How old are you?"

Suzie dissolves in giggles next to me while the uncles clap their hands and stomp their feet in glee.

I take my phone from my pocket to make sure no one has put any apps on it and notice there's a message from Ryker. He made sure I had his number programmed into my phone after our date at the pub a few days ago. Wait. No. It wasn't a date.

Do you want to go to the Packers game on Sunday?
"The Packers are football, aren't they?"

Everyone at the table freezes and then their gazes zero in on me. Oh no. What did I do wrong now?

"She's not from Wisconsin and she's a girly girl. Leave her alone," Suzie declares. "Besides, there are more important things to discuss. Why do you want to know?" she asks me.

I shrug. "I'm curious is all."

"Curious right after you checked a message on your phone? Sell it to someone else, sister, 'cuz this girl ain't buying it."

My face heats and I confess, "Ryker asked me to go."

Wally leans forward. "To Green Bay?"

"I don't know. Is Green Bay where they play?"

The men gasp and clutch their chests.

"What?"

Aiden explains, "The Green Bay Packers play football in Green Bay."

In Green Bay?

At least I can't see if Ryker thinks I'm a total idiot for asking.

Yes.

Ok.

I give him a simple answer even though I'm squealing like a little girl inside. This is definitely a date, right? Oh wait. I've sworn off men. Butterflies, clip your wings, we are not excited about going to the game with Ryker. They ignore me and continue to flutter away.

"We'll all go," Wally announces.

"How are you going to get tickets?" Aiden asks and then thinks better of it. "Don't tell me. I don't want to know."

Suzie claps. "We can tailgate."

"What's tailgating?" The question slips out before I realize I'm showing my ignorance again.

"It's awesome. You are going to love it. We're going to pop your tailgating cherry."

Um, she didn't answer my question.

Hailey leans forward, so I can see her. "It's basically a party in the parking lot of the stadium. Everyone brings food and drink."

"And we can barbeque. Do you still have your travel barbeque?" Suzie asks Pops.

I tap Hailey on the shoulder and motion to the restrooms. She stands and we sneak off while Suzie is chattering away making plans.

"Do I tell Ryker you guys are coming?" I feel like a complete and utter idiot. These are not questions other women have to ask.

"You don't have to, but you can casually mention the tailgate party and ask if he wants to go."

Why didn't I think of that? I nod my thanks and she smiles before walking back to the table. She barely makes it two steps before Suzie jumps in front of her.

"What are you guys whispering about? Is it a secret? Can I know? Tell me now."

Suzie's mouth motors away as she hops around. She looks back at me and winks as she turns the corner into the pub. Pops, carrying a tray piled high with dishes, tries to duck out of her way, but no one can avoid the maelstrom known as Suzie. She jumps straight into him. She bounces and skitters backwards before falling onto her bottom. The tray wobbles before Pops loses control. Dishes and bowls go flying. A bowl of cranberry sauce lands right on Suzie's chest.

She dips her finger into the sauce. "Mmm… yummy." She lifts her shirt and starts licking the mess off.

"You'll be wasting your breath," Hailey says before I can yell at Suzie for her unhygienic behavior.

"Is this normal?"

She giggles. "Aren't you used to Suzie by now?"

No one can get used to Suzie. Not really. "No, I mean there were fart jokes at the dinner table." And lots of people smiling in happiness. I've never seen people happy on the holidays before. Holidays are supposed to be stressful, aren't they?

"Oh yeah." Hailey giggles. "The uncles are probably already planning their Christmas prank. And Pops will want revenge as well." She winks. "You'll get used to it."

Get used to it? As in I'm invited to Christmas as well? My eyes itch and I have to look away before I give myself away. I blink fast and take deep breaths to stop the tears from falling. I've heard of happy tears before, but I thought they were a myth. I'm happy to ruin some mascara to bust this myth. Phoebe 2.0 – as I've now decided to call myself – has a rocking life.

Chapter 14

Accept a gift with grace. In other words, no bitching to go halfsies. ~ Phoebe's rules for becoming a better person

WHEN RYKER'S TRUCK APPROACHES my boarding house on Sunday, I'm standing outside on the sidewalk waiting for him. I'm not ashamed of how I live. Lie. I'm a little ashamed. Okay, fine. I was a lot ashamed when he looked around at my place in disgust.

"Princess," he calls as he approaches, and a shiver runs down my spine as butterflies take note and wake up in my stomach. I love it when he calls me Princess in his growly voice. "Why are you standing out here?"

"I was waiting for you."

"It's twenty-five degrees out."

Tell me something I don't know. "I'm all bundled up for the game."

Since Ryker invited me to the game, I've done some research on the Green Bay Packers and Lambeau Field. It's an outdoor stadium. Brrr… And there's me without thermal underwear. My previous life did not lend itself to situations where I would need thermal underwear. And it turns out thermal underwear isn't cheap. So, instead, I've dressed in as many layers of clothes as I can and still be able to zip my coat.

Ryker chuckles before taking my hand and leading me to the truck. "It's a two-hour drive. Unless you want to melt in the car, take a layer or two off."

I try to keep my eyes open as we drive out of the city and get onto the highway. I do. But it's toasty warm in the truck and I didn't sleep well last night, which is a bit of an understatement. Since the cold weather arrived in the city, I discovered the wind whips right through the window into my room. I sleep under several blankets, but I never get warm enough to relax and sleep. I fear I'm starting to develop a hunchback from hunching over in bed all night long.

"Princess," someone whispers into my ear. I groan and turn over. My head smacks against something hard.

"Ow!" I open my eyes to see we've arrived. My eyes widen as I take in the scene in front of me. Is this a parking lot? It's a huge party is what it is. People are milling about drinking beer and eating hotdogs. There are barbeques in the backs of trucks and people have set up tables and chairs to eat.

"This must be tailgating."

Ryker grins. "You've never been tailgating before?"

I didn't even know what tailgating was until a few days ago. Which reminds me. "Suzie and Hailey are out here somewhere. How do we find them?"

His grin widens. "Call them."

Once I've placed the call and Hailey has given Ryker directions to find where they are, we climb out of the truck. I shiver. Watching everyone walking around and partying, I forgot how cold it is outside. Ryker wraps his arm around me and pulls me close.

"I've got blankets and hand-warmers." He lifts a see-through bag he's carrying to show me.

"What are hand-warmers?"

"Babe," he grunts and kisses my forehead.

"Babe isn't an answer."

"Hotdogs! Get your hotdogs here!" I hear Suzie shout before we walk through another lane of cars and I can see her. "You made it!"

She runs toward us. A group of guys are throwing a ball around in the lane. They don't anticipate her running straight through their game area. Why would they? One of the guys throws the ball and it smacks Suzie in the head. She wobbles but somehow manages to catch the ball before it falls to the ground.

"Who threw this?" She glares at the guy who is now holding up his hands and backing away. "You call that a throw? Dude. You throw like a girl. This is how you do it." She holds up the ball and lets loose.

"Shit. Suzie can throw a ball." Ryker practically gawks at her.

I get a strange feeling in my stomach as I watch him admire her. It starts to burn as the stare goes on and on. Oh my god. Am I jealous? I shake my head. I can't be jealous. Ryker isn't mine to be jealous of.

Then, why is his arm wrapped around you keeping you close to his side? asks a little voice in my head. Stupid little voice is nothing but trouble. I ignore it.

Ryker leans over and kisses my hair before smiling down at me. "Your girl is a nut."

I roll my eyes as if I haven't a care in the world while my stomach goes from churning acid to hosting a forest of butterflies. Ryker is always a good-looking guy, but when he smiles and his green eyes sparkle, he's downright gorgeous.

My stomach rumbles and his smile dies. "I need to feed you."

He pulls me toward the group of uncles gathered around a small barbeque. He doesn't bother saying hello to anyone. He pushes his way through them to grab a burger off the grill and shoves it into a bun before slathering it with ketchup.

"Eat." He pushes the burger into my hand.

I'd argue with him I don't take orders from men anymore. But my stomach growls again reminding me I'm starving since I haven't eaten yet today. I take a bite and groan. Why I resisted eating this kind of food is beyond me. Burgers, nachos, all bar food is flat out delicious. Not to mention way cheaper than fresh vegetables in the winter.

My mother's voice tries to remind me junk food is for the common people and not a lady, but I shove the voice out of my head. I'm tired of giving my mother real estate in my head. It's about time I evicted her royal bitchiness.

Hailey and Suzie join me. "Here," Suzie says and shoves a beer into my hand.

I take a sip. "This is yummy. A new flavor?"

Suzie is a brewer. She owns the microbrewery *Shorty's Brewing Sensation.* For some reason, the loudmouth doesn't like to talk about her beer. She nearly lost it when Hailey told Aiden she made the *Short but Stout* beer he likes.

"It's my Shorty's Holiday Brew. It's spiced and sweet like a traditional holiday beer."

I take another sip. "I taste ginger and cinnamon."

She beams. "Exactly."

"You and Ryker seem awfully close." Hailey winks.

I have no idea how to respond. I want to be close to him. But I'm not sure how he feels. Whoa. *Phoebe, you don't want a man, remember?*

"Imagine the babies you'd make. You're beautiful, he's hot. You're a PI, he's a bounty hunter. Your kids would be the best looking mini-badasses at the daycare center."

And now I'm imagining a little baby boy with Ryker's stunning green eyes and curly brown hair. He'd be a total hellion and I wouldn't care one bit. I'd shower him with affection, unlike my own parents who never hugged me. A kiss on the cheek was the most affection I received from them and when I reached thirteen, the kisses became air kisses. In case there's any confusion, let me state this loud and clear – air kisses are not real kisses.

Ryker walks over to our group. "Princess, we need to go find our seats."

"He calls her princess." Suzie sighs and throws a hand over her forehead and pretends to swoon. Hailey may be the one who studied drama, but Suzie's the drama queen.

I ignore Suzie and grab the hand Ryker's holding out. I wave good-bye to everyone before we start walking to the stadium. I notice most of the crowd is packing up now, and lines are starting to form in front of the gates.

Everyone is laughing and joking. I can feel the excitement in the air. I'm getting excited myself. I've never watched a football game before. I tried to read up about it in the library yesterday, but how can an online article convey the excitement brewing in the crowd now? Easy answer. It can't.

The line moves at a steady pace and before I know it, we're walking through the inside of the stadium. Judging by how my eyes are bulging out, they're likely the size of flying saucers. There are stands everywhere. It's like a shopping mall. I try to take it all in, but Ryker is moving fast, pulling me along with him.

"I'll get you settled and then come back out to get us some beer."

I tug on his hand. "Why? I can stand in line with you and help you carry the beer."

He snorts. "You think I need help carrying beer?"

Um, no. But I don't want him to have to run around taking me to our seats and then back out here. The lines are super long as it is.

My eyes widen when I realize I'm being an ungrateful cow. "I'll buy the beer." Should I offer to pay for my ticket as well? He asked me to come, does that mean he pays for the ticket? This is all very confusing.

"You're not buying the beer. And you're not paying for your ticket."

Can he read my mind? "I didn't say a word about paying for the ticket."

"No, but you were thinking it."

"How much does a ticket cost?" I probably can't afford to pay anyway.

"Come on. Let's get some beer. Game should be starting soon."

Notice he didn't answer my question. I open my mouth to ask again, but he cuts me off.

"No, Princess. You aren't paying. End of discussion. Glare at me all you want. Hell, you can throw a hissy fit. I don't care. When I ask a woman out, I pay. End of discussion."

Wait. Does he mean this is a date?

He chuckles and places his hand around my neck before pulling me close. "Yes, Princess, this is a date."

"But we've never even kissed." I slap my hand over my mouth. Why did I say those words? I must be losing my grip on reality.

"Baby," he whispers and pulls me close. "There's nothing I want more than to taste those plush lips of yours."

"Okay." My voice sounds breathy because I'm dying to feel his lips on mine.

He stares at my lips for a moment before mumbling, "Fuck it." His head descends and his lips touch mine. I'm surprised to discover his lips are soft. My tongue reaches out to taste him. He growls and shoves his tongue into my mouth. He licks into my mouth and I tremble as his spicy, outdoorsy taste hits me. I grab hold of his biceps and hang on as he plunders my mouth.

I hear clapping and he rips his mouth away from mine to snarl at whoever's clapping. The clapping stops, but I don't see who it is. I'm too busy staring at Ryker as my body hums and heats. And there's definitely some tingling as well. I have never felt this way before. Certainly not after a mere kiss. What have I gotten myself into?

Chapter 15

Never turndown a free piece of cake. ~ Phoebe's rules for becoming a better person

I WALK INTO *YOU Cheat, We Eat* the next morning to find the place dark. Huh. Weird. I know I'm earlier than normal. Who can sleep when the man of your dreams kissed you silly before taking off for the night? Not me. I tossed and turned all night while dreaming about Ryker's mouth and wondering how good his mouth would feel on other parts of my body. Goosebumps break out and tingles erupt at the sexy thought.

Get it together, Phoebe. Time to work and earn some money so you can afford to live somewhere you don't have to share a bathroom with men who cut their toenails in the sink and leave the evidence just sitting there waiting for the next person who uses the room. I flip on the lights and walk to Suzie's desk.

"Surprise!"

I scream, drop my bag, and back away. After two steps, I twirl around and run full out to the door. Someone puts their arms around me and pulls me away from the door.

"Leave me alone!" I scream and thrash around.

"Phoebe! Phoebe! It's me. Hailey."

I open the eyes I didn't realize I'd squeezed shut to discover Suzie and Hailey staring at me like I've lost my mind. I think I have. "Sorry. You scared me."

"Yeah. I got that when you tried to claw me." Hailey holds out her arm and pulls up her sleeve to reveal scratch marks. "Good thing it's winter. If I was wearing short sleeves, I'd be bleeding."

"I'm sooo sorry." I'm such an idiot. I don't even know why I ran. They startled me and instinct kicked in.

"I wish I'd had my camera ready. I bet two women clawing at each would get like a million hits on YouTube."

Thank the powers that be Suzie didn't have her camera. I can't have my face showing up online. There's a reason I don't do social media. And it's not the lame excuse about fearing spyware I told these two. I haven't the first clue what spyware is.

"Ta da!" Suzie holds out an envelope.

"What's this?"

"Open it and you'll see."

I rip the envelope open to discover my test results from the Private Detective Exam. When Wally told me my background check was 'good to go', I couldn't complete my private detective license application fast enough.

"Ninety-five percent?" Hailey reads over my shoulder. "Phoebe's a genius. I barely passed with eighty-five percent." You need a score of eighty-four percent to pass.

"I'm proud of you," Hailey declares before engulfing me in a hug. Suzie joins us and makes it into a group hug.

I feel all warm and fuzzy inside and it's not because I passed the exam. No, this friendly hug is making me feel like I might have found a real friend. Two real friends in fact. Before these two, I never hugged my friends. Although based on how Hailey and Suzie act, I don't think those women can be categorized as friends. No, catty women who are only too eager to spill your secrets the second you're not around does not a friend make.

Suzie dislodges herself. "Plus, there's cake. Cake for breakfast!" She trips on air but manages to keep to her feet as she rushes to Hailey's office to grab the cake.

She dishes out slices of cake and we settle into the chairs in front of her desk to enjoy the chocolate goodness.

"I never thought I'd see the day," Suzie says with a shake of her head.

My lips turn down in a frown. I know I'm not your average PI, but I've been doing a good job here. Hell, I managed to get a picture of Stan Brown. A feat two investigators before me couldn't accomplish.

"Get rid of your frowny face. I'm not talking about you acing the PI test. You may be gorgeous, but you're no dummy." She points to my half-eaten piece of cake. "I'm talking about you eating cake. Not only eating cake but eating cake in the morning!"

At this point, I've learned to not refuse food, no matter how many gazillion calories it contains. I don't know why I still think about calories. Considering how many meals I skip, calories should be the least of my concerns. But counting the calories of every single morsel of food to enter my mouth is another habit my mother ingrained in me. Ugh. I need to research how to evict my mother from my mind because she is still living there rent free.

"Our girl's growing up." Suzie sniffs and rubs a finger under her eye to catch a nonexistent tear.

"Are you sure you're the one who studied drama?" I ask Hailey.

Suzie ignores my comment. "She's making jokes and everything."

"The uncles want to throw you a party," Hailey says.

"A party?"

"Don't worry." She grabs my hand. "It's just us, the uncles, and Pops."

I sigh. Thank goodness. I hate parties. Standing around making small talk with people I don't know or like while being put on display is not my idea of fun. I'm being silly. It will be fine. No one in Hailey's circle wears Dior gowns for parties. Their idea of a party is a fun night at McGraw's eating yummy food and drinking beer. No fake people allowed.

We finish our cake and I stand to start cleaning up before getting to work. I nearly drop the plates when Suzie asks, "And are you going to ask your hunka hunka burning love to the party?"

"He's not my…" What do I call him? Because *hunka hunka burning love* are words I plan on uttering never.

Before I figure out what I should call Ryker, Suzie continues, "Sure looked like he was your something something on the side when you two were making out in the Atrium yesterday."

My face heats. "You saw us."

"Everyone saw you, Pheebs. It's not like you were hiding."

I narrow my eyes. I told her not to call me Pheebs. It's undignified. My name is Phoebe. I swear I can hear my mother's voice telling me nicknames are for the help, not for us. Well, screw her. I am the help now.

Hailey hip checks me. "Call and ask him."

"Yeah, you're not chicken, are you?" Suzie clucks like a chicken and marches around the room in circles while flapping her arms like wings.

"I'll call him." Suzie raises her hand in triumph. "But not because you called me a chicken." I walk to my office and shut the door before anyone can follow me.

"You know I'm going to eavesdrop, right? There's no reason to shut the door."

I walk to the furthest corner of my tiny office and dial Ryker's number.

"Princess, is everything okay?" He answers on the second ring sounding out of breath.

"Yeah, but I think I'm disturbing you."

He chuckles. "Working out."

A vision of Ryker shirtless and sweating while lifting weights pops in my head. Do they have spectator bleachers at gyms? If not, they should. There's definitely a market there.

"Babe." Ryker's voice cuts into my vision of watching sweaty men playing volleyball. What can I say? I have an active imagination.

"Everything's fine. No, it's great. I passed my PI exam."

"I knew you would, sweetheart."

My face heats and my chest warms. Hearing Ryker call me sweetheart may be even better than him calling me princess. He's not one of those guys who throw terms of endearment out. Well, except for babe, which seems to be his favorite word. But babe is not a term of endearment.

"Anyway, we're having a little party at McGraw's tonight. Do you want to come?" I hold my breath. I've never asked a man out before. It's kind of terrifying. I'm not sure how men do this.

"Of course. I'll pick you up at your place at six." I hear grunting in the background. "Gotta get back at it. My sparring partner is getting anxious. See you tonight, Princess."

"Bye." My voice comes out all breathy. Of course, it does. Now I'm imagining Ryker shirtless while fighting another shirtless guy. Oh my. I'm starting to understand why women go gaga over MMA.

Chapter 16

Never underestimate your enemy. Lying, cheating scum that he is. ~ Phoebe's rules for becoming a better person

I RUSH OUT OF the door to the boarding house at five minutes to six. Ryker's truck comes around the corner and he pulls to a stop in front of the building. I skip to the passenger door with a smile pasted on my face. Whoa. Skipping? I'm turning into Suzie.

But someone got her first paycheck today. Sure, I've been paid by Hailey before, but it's always been cash. I never received an actual paycheck before. Imagine my disappointment when I didn't get an actual check. No, the money is directly deposited into my account. It kind of ruins the moment.

I jump in the truck and Ryker takes off.

"Seatbelt on, babe."

"Geez, someone's in a hurry," I grumble as I put on my seatbelt. "We don't have to be the first to arrive, you know."

Although I'm used to arriving fashionably late, I don't think the uncles will appreciate me showing up an hour late for my own party. And there's food. I am not going to be late for food.

It's strange how quickly food becomes an obsession when it's a rare commodity.

"You're going the wrong way," I point out when Ryker takes a left on North Broadway. "The pub's the other way."

He doesn't respond, but his hands tighten on the wheel until his knuckles turn white.

"What's going on?"

He still doesn't answer and now I'm getting worried. Should I have not invited him to the party? He could have said no instead of getting all angry.

"Why don't you drop me here?" I say as we stop at a red light. "You obviously don't want to go tonight. I can take the bus."

I reach for the handle and the locks click in place. "What the hell, Ryker? What is going on with you?"

He looks my way and the anger vibrating from his face has me scooting into the corner as far away from him as possible. "Your husband wants you back."

My heart stops as fear slams into me. "What? I'm not married."

"You can drop the act."

My hands start to shake as I realize he must know everything. All of my secrets. Was it all an act? The nicknames, the kiss, the date. Did it mean nothing to him?

The light switches to green and he slams his foot on the accelerator.

"I'm not going back to him. You can't make me."

"Babe," he snarls, and I snap. Who does he think he is?

"Oh, shut up with your babe and sweetheart and princess. I'm a job to you, nothing more." And man does the realization hurt. My heart burns. I reach a hand up to rub my chest.

I see the on-ramp for the interstate approach. Shit. If we get on the interstate, I'm lost. I have to get out of this truck. I slam my hands against the window and scream my head off. "Help! Help! He's kidnapping me."

"Babe, quiet down before I quiet you down."

I snort. He doesn't scare me. I've heard those words more times than he can imagine. "Fuck you." I add kicking the windshield to my escape attempt. I'm sure I look like a crazy lady, but I don't care. Hopefully, someone will see the crazy lady and call the cops.

"Someone help me!"

"I warned you," Ryker says, and then it's lights out.

I wake to discover myself lying in a bed with my hands bound together over my head. What the—? I pull on the cold steel of what must be handcuffs, but my hands aren't going anywhere since the cuffs are attached to the bedpost. Great. Just great. I try to pull myself into a sitting position but groan when my head and stomach decide movement is a bad idea.

I lay back down and survey the room. There's a bed with a scratchy bedspread, a table with two chairs, and a television mounted to the wall. Judging by the sound of cars flying by, we must be in a motel room right off of the highway.

When my stomach calms, I pull on the handcuffs again. The cuffs scrape against my wrists. Ouch.

"You're only going to hurt yourself." Ryker tilts his chin toward the cuffs as he approaches the bed to glare down on me. Like he cares if I'm hurt.

"I need the bathroom."

He chuckles, but it's not the sweet chuckle I was becoming addicted to. No, this sound is pure evil and full of the threat of danger. "Like I haven't heard that one before."

My stomach rolls. "Seriously. I need the bathroom."

He crosses his arms over his chest. "The next thing you're going to say is it's that time of the month. This isn't my first rodeo."

"What did you—" My question about what he gave me gets cut off when I lose the fight with my stomach. I lean my head over the side of the bed as far as possible and empty my stomach contents on the floor.

"Fuck." Ryker jumps back. He doesn't try to hide his look of disgust.

My throat is raw and there are now chunks of vomit in my hair. I gag as my hair sways into my face and the smell hits me. No contest. This moment is going in the top ten of my least favorite moments in my life.

The asshole steps over the puddle of vomit to unlock my handcuffs. Before I can cheer, he hauls me to my feet and drags me into the bathroom where he re-attaches one cuff to my left wrist and the other cuff to the towel rack.

"Clean yourself up." He dumps a plastic bag on the counter.

"Sure. Should be easy to do with one hand."

"Keep your mouth shut or you'll regret it," he says and slams the door shut.

Regret it? I was done hearing about how I was going to regret everything before I invented the new Phoebe. And now? Now, the new Phoebe is not going to regret a damn thing. Screw him. I'll figure out how to get myself out of this mess. I just need a plan.

In the meantime, there are chunks of vomit in my hair to deal with. I can't wait to try and wash my hair one-handed while handcuffed to a towel rack. Another experience to add to the least favorite moments in my life. I'm racking them up today. I open the plastic bag and discover a bar of soap, a can of deodorant, a hairbrush, and some hair bands. No shampoo. Of course not.

I hear the door to the motel room open. I abandon the bag and move as close as I can to the door. My shoulder aches as it's stretched to the absolute limit so I can lean my head against the door to eavesdrop.

"Thanks for coming. My wife got sick. She drank too much at our wedding and got alcohol poisoning."

I roll my eyes. As if anyone would spend their wedding night in this dump.

Someone – I assume the maid – giggles. "I'll get you cleaned up right away." I can hear how breathy her voice is. I snort. The man may look fine, but his heart is black and rotten. Total asshole territory.

I consider shouting, but what's the use? The maid already thinks I'm a drunk newlywed. Besides, she'd likely take Ryker's side anyway. I have an absolute ton of experience with women taking the side of a man, particularly my husband. That particular man is a total snake, but no one ever saw it.

I return to the sink and my hair problem. Shampoo or not, I have no choice. I switch the taps on and stick my hair under the water without bothering to wait for it to warm. I manage the best I can with one hand and no shampoo. When I'm finished, I brush out my hair and throw it into a messy bun. I'd worry about how tangled my hair will be in the morning, but I've got enough worries on my head.

I hear the maid leave the room. I hope she managed to get rid of the smell because I don't fancy sleeping in a room smelling of vomit.

Ryker opens the door and unlocks the cuff on the rack. He drags me to the bed and loops the cuff through the headboard and attaches it to my wrist once again. My stomach growls and his jaw tightens.

"I'll get you something to eat if you promise to shut the hell up."

Gee. Someone has forgotten his manners.

"I'll be quiet," I declare.

I'm starving and trying to think of an escape plan while I'm hungry won't work. Having a growly, empty stomach does not help with concentration. Another wonderful lesson I've learned over the past year, which I never considered in my previous life. Oh sure, I donated to charities that supplied food to the hungry, but I never once considered what it would be like to actually be hungry.

Ryker returns in less than five minutes with another plastic bag. He throws the bag at me and I tip the contents onto the bedspread. Looks like it's potato chips and soda for dinner. Oh, how my mother would cringe.

Shit. Mother. I'm going to have to see her again. And Father. Damn. My eyes burn, but I shut them before any tears can leak out. I am not going to show any weakness in front of Ryker the Asshole.

"How am I going to eat?"

I rattle the cuffs in case he doesn't get my drift.

He shrugs and walks off. "Asshole."

"What did you call me?"

"Asshole, because you are an asshole."

"I'm only doing my job, babe."

"Your job is to kidnap women and take them back to their abusive husbands? Good for you." Ryker's body freezes, but I'm on a roll and don't notice. "I thought you were my friend, but I'm just a job to you. I'm a person. Not a job. You're not a mere asshole. You're the king of assholes."

He's done listening to me. He switches on the television and increases the volume. "Try to get some rest. Tomorrow's a long day."

Because we're driving back to California. You can hardly take a kidnap victim on a plane after all.

Chapter 17

Never underestimate pissed off semi-family members with military training. ~ Phoebe's rules for becoming a better person

ALTHOUGH I FELL ASLEEP almost before I finished chewing the last potato chip, my sleep is fitful. Getting comfortable with my hands restricted is darn near impossible. My shoulders are starting to ache from the unnatural angle. I want to toss and turn but I don't have enough range of motion.

Ryker has none of my problems. He laid down on top of the scratchy bedspread while fully clothed – including shoes – and promptly fell asleep. It's unnatural. He's laying with his hands across his chest and his feet crossed and hasn't moved a muscle.

I stare at the clock attached to the television as it moves to 3 a.m. My head is full of thoughts on how to get myself out of this situation. I hate to admit it but escaping now doesn't seem like my best bet. I have no idea where we are. And, without any mode of transportation, Ryker would catch up to me in no time. And I can't get these cuffs off anyway. No, the best chance I have to escape is somewhere populated. Somewhere he has to deal with a bunch of strangers.

California is a long way away. We can't take backroads the entire time. The trip would take a week and there's no way Asshole Sleeping Next To Me Without A Worry In His Fat Head is going to put up with me bitching and moaning for a week. He'll be forced to take the interstate where the gas stations are usually full of travelers. He's going to have to let me go to the restroom at some point. All I have to do is get one person's attention and tell them I've been kidnapped.

Plan in place – such as it is – I close my eyes and finally drift off. I awake with a start when I hear a loud crash. I open my eyes to find the door to the room hanging off its hinges and Wally standing in the opening. Ryker jumps to his feet with a gun in his hand. Shit. Where did he get a gun?

"Don't shoot Wally," I scream.

Someone pulls on my arm. "Come on, Doll. Let's get you out of here."

I gawk at Lenny as he helps me to my feet. "But the handcuffs?" I wiggle my wrists and discover I'm free. "How did you—"

"Quiet, Phoebe," Sid orders.

Where the hell did he come from? I look around and notice Barney standing next to Wally. I guess the gang's all here.

Wally and Barney are in a standoff with Ryker. All three have their guns raised and pointed at each other.

"You can shoot me," Wally says with a smug look on his face. "But Barney will shoot you in return. You lost this round, kid."

"I knew you four were trouble the second I saw you."

Barney smiles. What a strange time to smile. "Five. But Pops couldn't make it." He looks my way. "He sends his regards."

"Um, thanks?"

"We need to get out of here before we attract attention." Wally motions with his pistol. "Are you going to be smart or dumb?"

I raise my hand. "I vote dumb."

Lenny puts his arm around me and pulls me close. "Let's go." He starts walking around the bed to the door with Sid in front of him.

Ryker growls and moves. He keeps his gun raised and pointed toward Wally but situates himself at the end of the bed, preventing us from leaving. "You can't take her."

And now, I'm done. "Can't take me! I'm not a commodity, you asshole. I'm a human being. I know the concept is strange to you since you're a Grade A Asshole who thinks he can take people against their will, but I will not be taken. I am not going back to the man who abused me. I'm not."

I look around the room. "Clue in. It's five against one. You can't win."

"Your husband wants you back."

I snort. "My husband doesn't want me back. He wants his perfect Stepford wife who makes him look good back. Tell him to buy one off Amazon, because I am not on the market."

"As much as I'm enjoying watching our Phoebe come into her own, this has gone on long enough." Wally nods to Barney.

The next thing I know Ryker is on the floor with Barney's knee in his neck. "How did—" I shake my head as I cut myself off. There's no sense asking a question I know these men won't answer. Still, when did jokester Barney learn how to take down a man twice his size?

I watch with my mouth gaping open as Barney hogties Ryker. Ryker fights him but Barney gags him and ties him up without breaking a sweat. I think I underestimated Hailey's uncles. I should have realized when she told me they taught her to shoot every weapon known to man, there was more to them than meets the eye.

Barney stands and wipes his hands on his jeans. "Let's go."

"We're just going to leave him there?" I don't know why I care. Oh wait, I do know. "We should call the police. The man is a kidnapper."

Sid raises an eyebrow. "Do you want to stay here and talk to the police? Give them a statement and explain every little detail about your past? About why your husband hired a bounty hunter to bring you back?"

I bite my lip and consider his questions. I know the right thing to do is call the police. But would calling the police prevent my dear husband from hiring another bounty hunter? "But what if he hires more men to come after me?"

Lenny's arm around me spasms. "No one is going to capture you and cuff you to a bed ever again," he vows and the rest of the uncles grunt in agreement.

"It's up to you," Sid says. "We won't take your choices away from you. You decide. Call the police or go home?"

I look to Wally. "What do you think?"

"I think calling the police will not make one bit of difference in what your husband does. I think Theodore Abbot does whatever the hell he wants and thinks he's above the law."

I gasp. He knows my husband's name? Of course, he does. I told him my real name after all. I'm sure he couldn't do a background check quick enough after I left his place once I'd revealed my real name.

And he's right. Theodore – never Teddy – does think he's above the law. Of course, I'd think I was above the law too if every time someone made a complaint against me, the complaint magically disappeared. It doesn't hurt to have friends in high places. Money can buy you friends anywhere. And I do mean anywhere.

I sag into Lenny's arm. "Okay. No police."

He kisses my hair. "Good choice, Doll."

"Let's get on the road. We've got a five-hour drive ahead of us." Wally walks out of the motel room and we follow.

As I pass Ryker, I'm sorely tempted to kick him in the balls. Unfortunately, he's laying on his stomach. I raise my foot, willing to settle for a swift kick up his rear, but Lenny pulls me away. "Not worth it."

"Says you."

When we walk out of the room, I'm shocked to see the parking lot is deserted. Either no one heard the rescue, or no one cares to stick their nose in other people's business. Considering how no one was willing to interfere when I was screaming my head off in Ryker's truck, I'm thinking it's the latter.

"How did you find me?" I ask once we're settled in the SUV. I'm laying in the back seat using Lenny's lap as a pillow with my legs draped over Sid.

Wally chuckles. "We have our ways."

I roll my eyes at Mr. Mysterious.

"We've had our eye on Ryker from the beginning," Sid says.

"Really? Did you not trust him?"

Sid snorts. "A bounty hunter interested in our Phoebe? The same Phoebe who is all secretive about her past? It didn't take much to add one plus one and get trouble."

Now they tell me. They couldn't have warned me about what a snake in the grass Ryker was. And why did he have to befriend me and kiss me? Couldn't he have kept his hands and lips to himself?

"Get some sleep, Doll. It's a long drive and you've had quite the day already." I want to argue with Lenny that I'm not tired, but he pets my hair and before I know it my eyes fall closed.

Chapter 18

Friends don't keep secrets from friends. ~ Suzie's rule for Phoebe becoming a better person

I WAKE WHEN LENNY squeezes my shoulder. "We're home, Phoebe."

I panic. Home? I don't want to be home. I thrash and kick out. Sid holds my feet down. "It's us, Phoebe. Your uncles. Hailey and Suzie are waiting with Pops at McGraw's."

Oh. We're not California then. I deflate. "Sorry."

"Nothing to be sorry about, darling." Sid squeezes my legs before lifting them to open the door and exit the vehicle.

I sit up and take a deep breath. Hailey and Suzie are going to insist I tell them every itsy bitsy teenie weenie thing about me now. I am not looking forward to this conversation.

"Come on." Lenny grabs my hand and pulls me out of the SUV.

Barney, Wally, and Sid are waiting at the door to McGraw's Pub. "You ready?" Wally asks. I shrug. How in the world could I ever be ready to share my deepest, darkest secrets with my newfound family? I may know every rule of society in existence, but none of them prepared me for this moment.

He looks me up and down. "You're stronger than you think," he declares and pushes the door open.

The uncles surround me as I walk into the pub. The place is deserted. I look at the clock. It's not yet nine a.m. No wonder the place is deserted. I feel like it's been weeks since I left the city, except it's been less than a day. Was it only yesterday evening that I was on my way here for a celebration?

Hailey and Suzie shout when they see me. They push the uncles out of their way to jump me and envelope me in a hug.

"Thank god you're okay. We were worried," Hailey says as she squeezes me.

Suzie agrees. "Good thing the uncles knew what to do."

Speaking of which. I extract myself from Hailey and Suzie. "Um. I don't think I thanked you guys." I place a hand on my heart. "From the bottom of my heart, thank you. I can't think about what would have happened had you not found me." A shudder runs through my body. I don't want to go back to my old life.

"You're welcome," Wally says while the rest of them grunt.

Pops approaches me and pulls me into a hug. "Welcome home, darling. Sorry I couldn't join the rescue operation."

"I understand."

He releases me but tags my hand and leads me to the table where the uncles and Hailey and Suzie are gathered. He forces me into a chair and takes a seat next to him.

"I hate to say it, but I think it's time for you to tell us all your secrets."

The door opens and I jump to my feet. Oh no, Ryker's back already. Pops grabs my hand and squeezes. "It's okay. It's Aiden."

I look to the uncles. "I thought we weren't involving the police."

"Aiden's not here as a police officer. He's here because he's your friend," Hailey explains. Aiden grunts in agreement as he lifts Hailey off her chair. He sits in the chair and pulls her into his lap.

"Where are we?" Aiden asks.

"Phoebe is about to tell us her secrets," Suzie says.

My eyes widen. "I never said I'd tell you my secrets." I'm sure Wally knows all he needs to know. No one else needs to hear my poor little rich girl story.

"Phoebe?" Aiden calls. He waits until I look at him before speaking, "Sorry to tell you this, sweetheart, but you have to tell everyone. I'm not being nosy. But the time to keep secrets has passed. Your husband not only knows where you are, he sent someone after you who used force to take you. If you think he won't use the people around you as pawns in his game, you're wrong."

My eyes widen as he speaks. Oh no, I hadn't considered how my situation could affect others. I stand. "Maybe I should leave." I've done it before. I can do it again. But instead of getting complacent, I'll keep moving. Every year – no, every six months – I'll move.

Aiden blocks my escape. "I'm not saying you should flee. I'm saying you should look to your friends. Let us help carry the load. Let us keep our eyes peeled for possible danger. But we can't help keep you safe if we don't know what danger we're facing."

Darn it. He's not wrong. I collapse in the chair. He makes a damn good point. Although I'm sure he knows all my secrets already. There's no way Aiden the Detective didn't sus out my past by now.

"It sounds stupid."

Suzie grabs my right hand and Hailey grabs my left. "Nothing about you is stupid," Hailey argues, and Suzie squeezes my hand in agreement.

I take a deep breath and dive in. "I'm sure you've all figured out by now I come from money. I don't mean to brag, but it's not a little money. My family is one of the wealthiest in the world. Sounds great, right?" I snort. "It's not. My parents don't care about me or my siblings. We are merely objects to them. Things they can use to advance their desires. In other words, make even more money. Case in point? They married me off to a man I didn't love."

Suzie gasps. "Couldn't you have said no?"

I shrug. "I didn't know any better. Don't forget. This is how I was raised. My parents don't love each other either. Their marriage was a business deal to merge two companies together."

"What happened?" Hailey asks.

"Well." I gulp. "It was hell." The uncles growl. "He didn't hit me if that's what you're thinking. But he controlled every detail of my life. Who I was allowed to socialize with. What clothes I could wear. How I should cut my hair. The color of my nail polish. He hired a personal secretary for me and then used her to control every single thing about me."

"Couldn't you divorce him?"

I shake my head at Suzie. "No. I mean, I did try, but the terms of the agreement stipulated we had to be married for a minimum of ten years. There's even a bonus for our fifteen-year anniversary. When I threatened to divorce him, he locked me in my room for two days. I may have had all the food I could eat and luxury beyond most people's means, but it was a prison nonetheless."

I pause before telling them why I finally left. "I learned to obey. I was a living doll. I had no thoughts of my own, except for one. There was no way I was having a child with Theodore. I was not subjecting a child to this life. Theodore had forbidden me from taking birth control but in this one thing, I defied him. But he found out. To say he wasn't happy is a massive understatement. I ended up in my luxury prison for two weeks. And the threats …" I trail off. Theodore more than threatened, but I fought tooth and nail.

Aiden takes my hand. "Phoebe, sweetheart. Did he force himself on you?"

"No." I shudder. "He … ah … found my struggling with him a turn-off."

"And then you ran away?"

"Not at first. I went to my mother and told her what was happening. She laughed in my face. Called me a poor little rich girl and told me to go back to my husband where I belonged."

"But you didn't."

"No, at first I did. After my mother sent me packing, I realized I had no support. It wasn't like I had any friends of my own I could trust. If I was going to run away, I needed a plan. I contacted one of the women I knew who worked for a charity helping abused women. Charity work was one of Theodore's requirements. It was important for his wife to be a 'do-gooder'. His words, not mine.

I knew he was watching everything I did, but there was nothing suspicious about me spending more time working with this charity. I was able to meet with my contact and concoct a plan. It was a simple plan really. I packed up all my clothes and told Theodore I was donating everything to charity. He approved since my clothes were too sexy for a thirty-year-old. With my car loaded up with the clothes I was 'donating', I met my contact who had a new identification with a new name waiting for me. I took off and never looked back."

There. I'm done. I have no more secrets to tell.

"And then you walked into *You Cheat, We Eat,* and we adopted you." Suzie always has to get the last word in.

"Why Phoebe answered your raucous ad is anyone's guess."

"It wasn't that bad."

Hailey rolls her eyes. "Did you forget about the hallway full of hookers?"

Suzie giggles. "No, it was awesome."

"Why do you think Theodore wants you back now?" Wally asks.

"Well, it's not because he loves me and misses me." When no one laughs at my quip, I sober and explain, "My leaving makes him look bad. Looking bad in front of the rest of society is nearly worse than losing all your money."

"Do you think he'll keep coming after you?" Aiden asks.

"No idea. I didn't think he'd send a bounty hunter to kidnap me." Damn Ryker. Why did he have to get close before taking me? Why did he make me think there are good men in the world before turning around and breaking my heart? No, I'm not heartbroken. He betrayed him. He didn't break my heart. Asshole.

"You're staying here until this matter is settled," Pops announces. "I've got the space and a modern security system. Plus, the place is almost always full of people who can keep an eye out."

"I don't want to put you out," I protest despite the idea of staying in a real bedroom where I don't have to worry about what happens when I need to go to the bathroom in the middle of the night being more than a little appealing.

"You're staying here or we're locking you up in a safe house until your husband is dealt with." My eyes widen at Wally's declaration.

"You wouldn't?"

"Darling, if I had known how you were living, I would have locked you up weeks ago."

My cheeks heat and my head drops to study the table. "I did the best I could."

Pops stands. "Now is not the time. Phoebe is dead on her feet. She needs to rest in a safe place." He holds out his hand to me. "Come on, darling. Let's get you situated."

My eyes itch at his friendly gesture. I sniff and take his hand. He squeezes and pulls me into another hug. "You're home, darling. No one can touch you here. I promise."

His words make me lose the struggle with my tears. Home. It sounds like a dream.

Chapter 19

Laughter and bacon makes everything better. Just don't forget the bacon. ~ Phoebe's rules for becoming a better person

WHEN I WALK OUT of Hailey's childhood bedroom into the kitchen, I'm surprised to see Hailey and Suzie sitting at the kitchen table whispering while drinking coffee.

"I didn't know you could whisper," I tell Suzie.

Hailey raises her hand for a high-five. "That's what I said!"

Okay, it's time to give this high-five thing a try. The Phoebe who doesn't high-five has left the building. I lift my hand and aim to smack Hailey's. I miss her hand almost completely. Instead of the sound of hands slapping together, there's a totally lame brushing sound as my hand glides off hers. I fail my first high-five test.

"You'll get the hang of it," Hailey says like it's no big deal a thirty-one-year-old doesn't know how to high-five.

My eyes fall upon the kitchen counter and widen at the plethora of breakfast food laid out. Good grief, there's more food here than a breakfast buffet at the country club. "Um… did the breakfast genie visit?"

Hailey joins me, grabs a plate, and starts piling it ahigh with pancakes, sausage, eggs, and waffles. "Pops cooks to show his love."

"Show his love?" What is she talking about?

She hip-checks me. "He's concerned about you."

Wait. What? "This is for me?"

Suzie joins us. "Well, it sure ain't for me. Not a donut in sight."

Hailey hands me the plate. "Here. Go sit down. I'll bring you coffee."

I nearly drop the heavy plate. "This is for me? I can't eat this much food."

"Maybe not. But you're going to try."

"I am? I'm going to try to fit all this food into my body?"

Suzie wrinkles her nose. "Haven't you stuffed your face before?"

"Ladies don't stuff their faces. In fact, we starve ourselves." Will I ever get the Wicked Witch of the West – aka my mother – out of my head?

"Screw that. Food's awesome," Suzie says and stuffs two pieces of bacon into her maw.

"She's not wrong." Hailey hands me my coffee and motions to the table. "Come on. Let's eat."

I take a seat and watch as Hailey and Suzie join me. I look at the clock. It's nearly four p.m. I must have slept most of the day. "Shouldn't you guys be at work?"

"Nope," Suzie says letting the P pop.

"Um, it's Wednesday. Isn't the office usually open until 5:30?"

Hailey lays a hand over mine. "This is what girlfriends do."

There's no sense holding back the truth. They know about my past now anyway. "I've never had girlfriends. At least not girlfriends who cared about me."

Suzie snorts. "Yeah, we kind of figured considering your great reveal and all."

Great reveal? Leave it to Suzie to make me tearing my heart out and telling my deepest dark secrets into something trite.

"She doesn't mean to be an idiot. It just happens."

"I'm not the idiot," Suzie argues. "Who was the one who didn't have the first clue how to comfort a girlfriend?"

"So, sue me. I don't like to sit around and talk about my feelings all the livelong day. That's why tequila was invented."

I clear my throat. "This is your idea of cheering me up?"

Suzie shakes her head. "Not exactly. According to the playbook, we first have to ply you with a thousand questions about your past until you bawl like a little baby. Then, when you're all cried out, we sit around and watch movies while drinking and eating too much."

A thousand questions about my past? I said about all I've got to say about my past last night. Or was it this morning? Time gets distorted when you're drugged by the man you think you're falling for, only to wake up and discover he's a monster. Asshole.

"You're growling." Hailey points at me with her fork. A piece of pancake goes flying and lands on the table. Suzie scoops it up and stuffs it into her mouth.

"Mmm… does your dad make his own maple syrup? This is better than anything I can find in the store."

"He uses honey and maple extract."

Suzie licks her lips. "It's awesome. He should bottle it up and sell it." She turns her attention to me. "Tell us all about this domineering husband of yours."

I'm getting whiplash from this conversation. "I'm not talking about Theodore." And I'm not calling him my husband. In fact, since he knows where I am now, I might as well file for divorce. And boy is that going to piss him off, even more than Ryker failing. I growl. Stupid Ryker.

"Uh oh. I think she's about to blow." Suzie leans back in her chair as if afraid of the blowback. The chair tilts back and Suzie disappears as it tips over.

Hailey ignores her best friend flipping over her chair at the table to ask, "Why were you growling?"

I do not want to talk about Ryker. But maybe this is what girlfriends do. They talk about the hard stuff. "Ryker."

Hailey frowns. "Yeah, he had us all fooled. Well, except for the uncles. But he had me fooled for sure. I really thought he liked you."

Suzie sighs as she sets her chair back on the floor and sits down. "He looked at you like you hung the moon."

"I don't get it. He's working for Theodore. Why didn't he kidnap me and be done with it? Why befriend me and think we share something special? Why kiss me?"

Hailey sighs. "Tell us about the kiss."

I wrinkle my brow. "Do I have to remind you he kidnapped me?"

Suzie slashes a hand through the air like the kidnapping was some kind of misunderstanding. "But was it a good kiss? Did it make your girly parts weep?"

I ignore her. "Was she born like this or do you think too many falls lead to brain damage?" I ask Hailey.

She snorts. "Sorry to disappoint you, but she's always been like this."

If I think I've managed to maneuver the conversation away from my relationship with Ryker, I'm proved wrong when she leans forward and squeezes my hand. "There's no shame in admitting you liked Ryker, you know. We girls have been known to let our hormones guide our actions."

I didn't think I was letting my hormones guide anything. I thought I was being careful and taking it slow. I guess I was wrong.

"Anyway," Hailey clears her throat, "I have an announcement."

"You're pregnant!" Suzie squeals and jumps to her feet. She tackles Hailey and they end up on the floor wrestling.

"I'm not pregnant. Get off me, you big oaf." Phoebe pushes Suzie away from her and stands. She brushes off her hands on her jeans before sitting again. "And when I do get pregnant, maybe try not to tackle me to the floor."

Suzie stays on the floor and tilts her head. "Oh yeah. Good advice."

"What's the announcement?" I ask before Suzie can tackle anyone else.

"I've picked a wedding date. And you both are bridesmaids!"

Suzie jumps to her feet and steps toward Hailey who throws her hands up in front of her. "No more tackling. I'm not a football player."

Suzie's shoulders slump for a second before she brightens back up. "Are you going to let us pick the bridesmaid's dresses?"

"Wait a second!" I hold my hand up to quiet the craziness. "You're asking me to be a bridesmaid? But—"

"Stop! You're my friend. One of my best friends." Suzie growls at Hailey's proclamation. "Definitely my only sane friend." Suzie shrugs before bobbing her head in agreement. "Of course, you are one of my bridesmaids."

"And no, you can't pick the dress," she tells Suzie. "I'm going to find the most hideous lime green dress I can find. Of course, this one…" She thumbs her finger at me. "… will still look beautiful."

"You couldn't have found a hideous looking friend to stand next to me at the wedding?"

"I'll get right on it. Right after we finish cheering Phoebe up."

I nearly jolt when I realize they did cheer me up. When I woke up in Hailey's childhood bedroom, I didn't think I'd ever smile again. Yet, here I sit with a big grin on my face laughing at Hailey and Suzie's antics. Suzie looks over at me and winks. Huh. Maybe she's not the oblivious crazy person she pretends to be.

Chapter 20

When crazy comes to town, call the police. ~ Phoebe's rules for becoming a better person

I PULL off MY gloves when I arrive at work the next morning. Huh. These are the gloves Asshole Ryker bought me. Why did he bother buying me gloves? The exact gloves I needed? Oh wait, he probably didn't. He must have expensed the so-called gift with Theodore – Asshole Number 2.

I throw the gloves into the garbage can. I don't need any reminders of the backstabbing men in my life.

"Hey! What are you doing?" Suzie reaches into the garbage can and pulls the gloves out. "These are perfectly good gloves."

"They're yours now." I march into my office before she can start asking her nosy questions.

"Do you want me to send Lola in to cheer you up?" She cackles in delight.

I flip her off. I know. I know. It's not polite, but she can't see me, so it doesn't count.

"Don't forget you have a prospective client coming in ten minutes!" she shouts through my closed door.

Fifteen minutes later, the outer door bangs open and the alarm beeps. Guess my ten o'clock has arrived.

Suzie opens my door with a flourish. "This is Ms. Adams." She winks at me. As if knowing my name isn't really Adams is some big secret. Not anymore it isn't. "She'll be happy to help you."

I smile at the woman hovering in the doorway and stand to walk around my desk. I hold my hand out to her. "It's nice to meet you, Ms. ...?"

She sneers at my hand before telling me, "You can call me Jenny."

I drop my hand and motion to the chair. "Please, have a seat."

"I'll stand."

"Of course." I walk behind my desk and stand in front of my chair. It's rude to sit when someone remains standing. I may have left my mother and her rules about being a lady behind, but I am nothing if not polite. "How can I help you today?"

Jenny, obviously not her real name, wrings her hands. I look closer and notice her fingernails are broken and a few are bleeding. I examine the rest of her. Her hair is in a messy ponytail. Her jacket is stained, and her jeans are full of holes. The poor woman looks like she's been put through the wringer.

"I'm being followed."

"Do you know who's following you?" I'm thinking a husband or jilted lover. After all, men are not to be trusted.

She shakes her head. "No. It's always a different person in a different car."

I admit it. I'm confused. "Then, how do you know they're following you?"

"Because they're stealing my ideas!"

Obviously, I've missed some information here. Time to back up. "Start at the beginning. What types of ideas? And how are they stealing them?"

Is this an intellectual property matter? Intellectual property is an area I have knowledge of, thanks to Daddy and Mommy dearest and their lovely lectures about the family pharmaceutical company. According to my parents, there's always someone trying to steal the latest miracle pill idea. Notice I said idea and not formula because none of those miracle pills work. Well, except to fill the company's coffers with money.

"The dentist planted a listening device in my crown."

"Um, okay. Why would the dentist do this?"

"Why?" she shouts. "Because he's in on it. Maybe you're in on it too." She narrows her eyes and glares at me.

I raise my hands in surrender. "I promise. I'm not in on it." I don't have the first clue what 'it' is. "Maybe you could explain what types of ideas they're stealing and how they're stealing them."

"My ideas are worth millions. I can design a vehicle that will not only fly but float on the water. Plus, it's completely self-guided since most people are idiot drivers."

"Are you an engineer?"

"No, I'm a graphic designer, but you don't need to be an engineer to design a vehicle."

I don't agree with her, but I have no desire to get into an argument with Ms. Paranoid.

"And how is someone stealing your ideas? Are they stealing your plans from your house?"

"I'm currently between homes and the ideas are all up here." She taps the side of her head with her finger.

Dare I ask how the ideas in her head are being stolen? Yes, I do. "And someone is stealing these ideas right out of your head?"

"Yes! I told you! From the listening device the dentist put in my tooth!" she shouts and starts pacing. There's not much space to pace in my office – two steps in either direction and you hit wall – but that doesn't stop her. She stomps two paces, raises her fist in anger to the wall, and then turns around to stomp in the other direction. "No one understands. No one believes me."

My phone buzzes. *Hailey's on her way in to help.*
I'm not sure what help Hailey can possibly be, but I definitely need help here.

"Why don't you take a seat and I'll get you a glass of water?"

"Water! You want me to drink water? You'll steal my ideas, too. I knew I couldn't trust you!" She rushes out of the room and runs smack dab into Aiden. I've never been happier to see the hunky man.

Jenny starts kicking and screaming, "Let me go! Let me go!"

Aiden twirls her around and slaps cuffs on her before pushing her into a chair. "Sit. Calm down."

I don't know what they teach at the police academy, but step one in dealing with a crazy woman is don't tell her to calm down. Jenny jumps to her feet and starts running at Aiden with her head down. Is she trying to tackle him? Thanks to my trip to the Packers football game, I now know all about tackles.

Dammit. Now, I'm thinking about Ryker again. I need a magic spell to evict him from my head. Why hasn't anyone invented a pill for evicting thoughts of asshole men from your head yet? I'd buy one. Hell, at this point, I'd sell my cherished Louboutins to afford it.

Aiden is six-foot-three and Jenny is around five-foot-five. She has no chance against the fit detective. He evades her with a step to the side. When she passes him, he grabs her upper arm and forces her back into the chair. He brings out a zip tie and connects her cuffs to the rear frame of the chair with it.

"Stay still or you'll hurt yourself," he orders. He motions for me to proceed him before backing out of my office and shutting the door.

"I take it we don't have a new client then," Suzie says.

"Why do I get all the crazies?"

Hailey pats me on the shoulder. "It comes with the territory. Remind me to tell you about the crazy cat lady over beer one of these days."

"What happens now?"

"I'll call it in," Aiden answers. "See if we can get her involuntarily committed."

"Committed." I gulp. "Like to a mental institution? You can't have her committed against her will, can you?"

Theodore has threatened more times than I can count to have me committed. It's one of my biggest fears. I bite my lip and my eyes drift to my office where I can hear Jenny mumbling to herself.

Aiden gets right up in my space. He grabs my jaw and forces me to look at him. "This is nothing like what your asshat of a husband tried to do to you." How does he know? "It's written all over your face." He takes a breath and lets it out. "Jenny needs help. We're not trying to hurt her. We're trying to help her." I nod and he drops his hand and steps away.

The uniformed police arrive and immediately take over. One of the officers asks me for a statement and before you know it, I'm caught up in the whirl of the police machine. It takes several hours to fill out all the necessary paperwork. By the time they leave, I've missed lunch. I'm hungry and tired.

As soon as the door closes behind them, I glare at Suzie. "You need to start screening potential clients."

"Sorry. Not sorry. Jenny needs help. Big time. And now she's going to get it," she says and flounces off.

Hailey puts her arm around my shoulders. "Why don't you quit for the day and head back to Pops' place?"

I'm not arguing with her. This week has been hell. Everyone always says the weeks between Thanksgiving and Christmas are busy. They have no idea. Between a kidnapping and the crazy woman, I'm exhausted.

I stand. "If you don't mind, I'm going to take the SUV to my place to pick up some clothes before I go to Pops'."

"Are you sure it's safe? I can come with you." In case I miss how Hailey will protect me, she pulls her gun out of her drawer. "I got ya."

"I already cleared it with the uncles. I think they're keeping a watch on my place in case Ryker or anyone else stops by." Stops by? Snort. Hunts me down is more like it.

I sound full of confidence as I convince Hailey I'll be totally fine. I'm not. But sounding confident and putting on a brave face were some of the first lessons my mother taught me. I learned them well. So well, in fact, I'm barely shaking as I walk toward my building scared out of my mind. What if Ryker is waiting for me? What if some other bounty hunter is after me? I wouldn't put it past Theodore to hire dozens of them to chase me. Money is no object after all.

The door to the boarding house is locked when I reach it. Thank goodness. I unlock the door and climb the steps to my room on the second floor. It's surprisingly quiet in the building. I guess mid-afternoon is when the junkies sleep.

I walk to my room with my keys out and at the ready. My feet speed up the closer I get. I got this. Wait. What's this? There's a package laying on the floor leaning against my door. No, I don't got this. I spin around screaming my head off as I run out of there like my ass is on fire.

Chapter 21

Fool me once, shame on you. Fool me twice and obviously, I'm a fool. ~ Phoebe's rules for becoming a better person

I TEAR OUT OF my building and run smackdab into Lenny. He grabs me and pulls me aside to allow Barney, Wally, and Sid to fly past us up the stairs.

"What happened, Doll?"

"Present. Door." I'm out of breath and can barely get the words out.

He rubs circles in my back. "Take a deep breath. You're safe. No one is going to harm you ever again."

Wally walks out of the building holding the package and I rear back. "What is it? It's not a bomb, is it?"

Wally chuckles. "It's not a bomb, kid."

Sid sticks his head out of the door. "Go ahead. We're going to pack up a suitcase for Phoebe." He winks at me. "You all right with that?"

I nod. Maybe I should be worried they're going to rummage through my underwear drawer, but Sid and Barney touching my unmentionables is the least of my worries at the moment.

Wally and Lenny escort me to a truck and then drive me to the pub. They usher me into their booth where Suzie and Hailey are already waiting. "How did you get here this quick?"

"Please." Suzie snorts. "You've driven with Hailey. Surely, you realize what a speed freak she is."

Hailey squeezes my hand. "Wally called us."

When did he possibly have time to call them? "Is he a ninja or a super secret governmental soldier or what?"

"I know, right?" Hailey bobs her head in agreement. "Ask me about the time I saw the lot of them disappear into thin air. I swear it was like 'Poof! Where did they go?'"

"What was the present?" Suzie asks.

I glare at her. "One of these days your curiosity is going to get you hurt."

"Nothing wrong with being curious."

"Yeah, sure, the proverb about curiosity killing the cat was invented for no reason."

Lenny, Sid, and Wally join us at the booth. Lenny is still carrying the present. I scoot as far away from it as possible. I want nothing to do with it.

"You're all set, Phoebe. We packed up two suitcases full of clothes and put them in your room upstairs," Sid announces.

"My room upstairs? It's not my room." I'm only staying at Pops' place until my life calms down.

Pops arrives. "It's your room for as long as you want it."

"We'll go back tomorrow and get the rest of your things packed up. Is the furniture yours?"

I hold up my hand. "I live there. You can't pack me up. Where will I live?"

Pops sighs. "I thought we already settled this." He sets a mug down in front of me. "Drink this. It will help your nerves."

I take a sip of the warm drink and nearly gag. "What did you do? Pour an entire bottle of whisky in here?" I manage to ask between coughs.

Pops winks before sauntering back behind the bar.

Barney joins us. "What did the hurricane say to the coconut tree?"

My eyes widen at him. Are the uncles completely unphased by today's events? I wish I could say the same for me but receiving a surprise package in front of my door days after being kidnapped is not an 'ordinary' day. Who would be crazy enough to want it to be?

"Hold on to your nuts. This ain't no ordinary blowjob." Barney guffaws and holds his fist up for Hailey who bumps his fist.

"I hate to say it, kid. But we need you to open the present." Wally shoves the package in my direction.

"Nuh-uh. No way. You open it." I shove the package right back at him.

"No. It's addressed to you."

I put my hands up to prevent him from giving me back the gift.

"I'll open it!" Suzie shouts before grabbing the gift off the table and tearing the wrapping paper off. "Well, that's disappointing. I was hoping for edible undies at least."

My upper lip curls. Edible undies. Those two words should never be said in the same sentence, let alone put together into a product.

Suzie slides the box my way. It's a bottle of Stolichnaya vodka.

"There's a card here, too." She holds up the tiny card. "All it says is *I'm sorry*."

"Could it be from your husband?" Lenny asks.

I glare at him. "I don't have a husband."

"Okay." He gives in. "Is it from Theodore?"

I shake my head. "Theodore has no idea I drink vodka martinis, let alone what vodka I prefer to drink."

"Which leaves Ryker." Wally grunts. "How the hell did he get into the building without us seeing? We've had the place watched since we brought Phoebe back."

His words do not instill confidence in their ability to keep me safe despite their undeniably impressive rescue operation. Maybe it's time for me to run.

Sid growls. "You're not running."

I throw my hands in the air. "How can you possibly know what I'm thinking?"

He smirks. "Like I don't know what a woman looks like when she's about to take off."

Suzie giggles. "Yeah, the man is an expert in the 'look'."

Sid slaps her shoulder, but he doesn't contradict her. "We got you. You're safe here."

"I can't deny I'm impressed with his skills, though," Wally adds.

I roll my eyes. Are they seriously crushing on Ryker's ability to get past them unseen? The same man who kidnapped me?

"I think your uncles are crazy," I tell Hailey.

Her eyebrow raises. "You're only figuring this out now?"

We spend the rest of the evening eating and drinking with the uncles. By the time Pops walks me up to the apartment several hours later, I'm feeling all warm and fuzzy inside. I may be a little tipsy. Another rule of my mother's I've broken – never get tipsy in public. I am done with her and her stupid rules. Screw her!

Pops leaves me with a kiss on my forehead. I walk into Hailey's childhood bedroom to discover two of my suitcases on her bed. All of Hailey's childhood memorabilia have disappeared. I walk to the dresser and open a drawer. It's empty. I pull all of the drawers open to discover each one is empty. I move on to the closet. It's also been emptied.

I collapse on the bed. My phone beeps and I grab it out of my pocket to read the message.

It's your bedroom now.

I can't accept this. I text Hailey back.

Too late.

The phone rings as I'm texting my response. I don't look at the caller ID. Big mistake.

"Princess."

I jolt upright and start running to the front door of the apartment. "I'm not your princess and you need to leave me alone."

"I screwed up."

"You screwed up?" I hiss. "How? You underestimated the uncles?"

"I should have never taken the job for your husband."

"I don't have a husband," I growl. Why am I talking to Ryker? I am done with him. "Leave me alone or I'll tell the uncles you're bothering me."

"I need to tell you something."

Suzie isn't the only one who's curious. "Then tell me."

"Not over the phone. You need to hear this in person."

In person? Yeah, right. "I may be blonde, but I'm not completely stupid. I'm not giving you another chance to take me back to Theodore. Call me again and I will tell the uncles."

"Pri—"

I don't hear the rest of what he has to say because I hang up. My heart is pounding, and my hands are shaking. I collapse on a kitchen chair and lay my head on the table.

When will this be over? Will Theodore ever let me go? Maybe I should move to another country. Canada is supposed to be nice. I'm sure I can find some isolated village somewhere. Somewhere a snake in the mud bounty hunter would be noticed the minute he showed up.

I still have some jewelry I can sell. Jewelry I've been holding on to for a rainy day. Well, guess what, it's pouring outside. I stand and go in search of my laptop. Time to research and make a plan.

Chapter 22

Always hear a person out. Unless he's a jerk.
Feel free to ignore jerks. ~ Phoebe's rules for
becoming a better person

"Ugh," I complain to Hailey as we walk into her dad's bar. "It's boring enough sitting outside someone's house all day waiting for them to mess up, but now I've got a group of old men following me as well."

"Who you calling old?" Sid asks as he follows us into the bar. "I'm in the prime of my life."

Hailey leans in close. "Rumor has it he has wife number six on the hook."

"Six?"

Sid pushes past us. "I told you, I've only been married four times."

"And I've told you, common law marriage is still marriage," Hailey shouts after him.

I shudder and feign gagging. "Being married once was quite enough for me. Five times? No way, Jose."

Hailey flashes her left hand at me. "I don't know. I'm willing to give it a try."

I snort. "Of course, you are. Mr. Perfect Detective is your future husband." I'm not jealous. No, really, I'm not. Being around someone as perfect as Aiden would drive me bonkers. I'm done with perfect people. Blech.

We join the uncles at their corner booth. They make way for me until I'm secured in the middle of them. They've been doing this a lot since I was kidnapped. Making me feel safe in simple ways. Unlike the people in my former life, they don't brag when they help me. No, they make me safe and carry on with their business. They make me feel cared for. It's a heady feeling after being brought up in my family.

Pops sets a martini and a shot of tequila in front of me. I raise my eyebrow at him. The martini I get. I always drink vodka martinis but the tequila? What's up with that? He leans over to kiss my hair. "So, you know, I was against this idea."

I freeze. "What idea?"

He moves and Ryker appears. I scream and scramble to my feet to run away. The uncles pin me down. Holy shit. They weren't being protective putting me in the corner, they were being pro-active. I glare at them. If I could shoot lasers from my eyes, they would be dead now. Stone cold dead.

"Traitors," I hiss.

And I know a thing or two about traitors. None of it good. My eyes swell and I sniff. I will not cry. I will not. It doesn't matter the family I thought was coming to love me betrayed me. I was planning on leaving anyway. I've already researched where to sell my jewelry and picked out a sturdy car to buy. I even have an idea of what village in Canada I'll be hiding out in.

"You are not running away," Wally hisses.

"I'll run away if I damn well want to. You are nothing to me. Nothing."

He flinches at the venom in my voice, but I don't care. He's breaking my heart.

"Move," Pops orders. When Sid doesn't get out of his way, he pulls Sid up by his shirt and throws him out of the booth before taking over his place. He places an arm around my shoulders and pulls me close. "I don't agree with these asshats, but you need to listen to what Ryker has to say."

I hide my face in his shoulder. "Why?"

"Darling, I wouldn't allow this if it wasn't important." He squeezes my shoulder. "Be the brave woman I know you are."

Me? Brave? I'm a chicken shit intent on running away as soon as I get a chance.

"Princess," Ryker says, and I growl.

"I am not your princess!"

He holds his hands out in a placating gesture. "Sorry. Can I sit down, please?"

I open my mouth to tell him he most definitely cannot sit down. In fact, he should get his ass out of the bar and leave the state. I've got enough assholes in my life – I glare at the men at the table – I don't need another one.

But Wally answers before I get the chance. "Please, sit."

I snarl as Ryker takes a chair.

The door to the bar bangs open and Suzie enters. "I'm home!" she shouts before skipping to us.

When she sees Ryker, her eyes widen. She rushes to him. As soon as she's within arm's reach, she lifts her bag and slams it down on his head. Good thing he's sitting down. The munchkin would never be able to reach the giant's head otherwise.

"How dare you?" She hits him again. "You hurt our girl!" Another hit.

She raises her arm to clobber him with her bag again, but Sid pulls her into his arms. "Calm down, crazy girl. Ryker has important information to share."

"How are friends like condoms?" Barney asks, and I look at him like he's lost his mind. Does it look like now is the time to make stupid jokes? He ignores my withering look. "They protect you when things get hard."

Hailey giggles and high-fives him. When I glare at her, she shrugs. "What? It was funny. You'll laugh later."

I don't plan on laughing again in my life. Ever.

Sid wrestles Suzie into a chair. "Can everyone calm down and listen to the man now?"

"How do you know what he has to say is important?" I sit back and cross my arms over my chest. There. Take that!

Lenny scratches his beard. "He came to see us this afternoon."

"What?" The men cringe at the high pitch of my voice. "You talked to him? Why didn't you arrest him? Or, I don't know, throw him in a dark cellar he could never escape from?"

Aiden clears his throat as he joins our group. Oh good, the gang's all here to watch my humiliation. Yippee. "Please don't tell me if you decide to do anything of the sort. And don't get caught."

Wally sniffs. "As if we'd get caught."

Ryker's being awfully quiet. I glance over to see his gaze is on me. His eyes are full of regret. Nope. I shake my head. I'm seeing things. The big bad bounty hunter regrets nothing. I narrow my eyes at him before pulling my gaze away.

He clears his throat. "Can I talk to Phoebe alone?"

Pops snorts and his arm around my shoulders spasms. "You're lucky you're here. If you think you can talk to my girl alone, you are wrong."

"I don't care what he has to say. He has done our girl wrong. He's out." Suzie stands in front of him with her arms crossed over her chest. Someone must have taken her bag away from her.

Hailey pulls on Suzie's arm. "He's not Toby, Suzie."

Toby is Suzie's ex. He put the A in asshole. He hurt Suzie to the point she's given up on men. She hasn't dated a man in years according to Hailey.

"No," Suzie snaps. "He kidnapped our girl."

"Thank you!" I clap. "Finally, someone remembers."

"I was wrong, okay?" Ryker shouts and pulls his hands through his hair. "Your husband—" I growl. He raises his hands. "Sorry. Theodore fed me all this shit about you being a spoiled little rich girl and I bought it."

"Clue in! Even if I were a spoiled little rich girl having a hissy fit, it doesn't give you the right to forcefully take me against my will."

His head drops. "Fuck."

"And if I'm just a spoiled rich girl, why not kidnap me at the start? Why pretend to be friends with me? Why kiss me?" Him kissing me and making me feel all kinds of things I've never felt before is what slays me. I know I'm crazy. Kissing me bothers me more than him kidnapping me. Obviously, I've lost my grip on sanity.

"I couldn't not kiss you. You look up at me with those green eyes and plush lips and I lose all control."

Suzie sighs and I glare at her. "What? It's romantic."

"Says the woman who thinks men are scum."

She shrugs as if she's not the world's biggest hypocrite.

Ryker interrupts our stare-down. "I need to tell you something."

Pops squeezes my shoulder. "It's important."

I nod. If the man who was willing to let me move into his apartment into his daughter's bedroom says it's important, I'll listen.

"Your—" He clears his throat. "Theodore doesn't want you back because he refuses to give you a divorce. He ... um ... needs you to have his baby."

"I know he wants an heir. This is not news."

"No, you don't understand. In the terms of the agreement between your parents and him, if you have a child and produce a grandchild for your parents, he gets a large amount of money."

"How much money?" Nosy Suzie asks.

"A shit ton. Seven figures."

"Now I know why he went ballistic when he found my birth control pills."

Ryker growls. "Ballistic?"

I roll my eyes. "Dude, you don't get to be angry on my behalf. I'm the spoiled little rich girl, remember?" And now I'm on a roll. "You saw where I lived. How could you possibly think I was spoiled or rich for that matter? The things I saw in the shared bathroom." I make a disgusted face. "And I couldn't even afford to live in that hellhole. I had to beg for money from Wally."

"What? Why didn't you tell us?" Hailey asks and Suzie nods in agreement. "We could have given you an advance."

"I needed Wally's help with other things as well."

Ryker looks at Wally. "You're the one who did the background check? When Theodore saw someone digging into his past, he told me to grab her."

Wally frowns. "I figured as much." He reaches across the table and squeezes my hand. "I'm sorry, Phoebe. I swear I was careful, but when you have those kinds of funds…"

"Yeah, I know. Money talks."

"What's the plan?" Aiden asks.

Ryker looks at Wally who nods in encouragement. "I need to convince Theodore Phoebe died."

"Will he believe you?"

"There's no reason not to. I'll fake an accident report. I'll say she died when she ran out of my truck into traffic and was hit by a car."

Geez. Do I have to die in such a brutal manner?

"I've got it." Ryker starts to protest at Wally's declaration, but Wally holds up his hand. "You know I have the contacts to make this look more authentic than you can."

Wally looks at me. "You okay with our plan, kid?"

Do I have a choice? "As far as I'm concerned, Phoebe Abbot never existed." I'm not lying. Phoebe Adams, aka Phoebe 2.0, is the real me. Phoebe Abbot was merely the practice round.

"In the meantime, we'll continue to protect Phoebe," Lenny declares.

"You mean follow me," I grump.

Chapter 23

I MOVE THE CURTAIN aside to look outside the window. I sigh before moving back to sit on the couch in the bridal boutique.

"This is ridiculous. First, he kidnaps me. Now, he's going to be my protector. Yeah, right."

Suzie leans her cheek on her clasped hands and does an exaggerated sigh. "I think it's romantic."

"You don't believe in romance, remember?"

She shakes her head. "I don't believe in romance for me. For other people? I'm all for it."

"You do realize you described a hypocrite."

Hailey sighs. "Don't bother wasting your breath. Suzie has her own definitions for things. I've tried buying her a dictionary. It didn't make a damn bit of difference."

"I think you should give him a second chance."

I ignore Suzie and speak to Hailey. "You're not kidding. Her grasp of the English language is abysmal."

"I know what a second chance means," Suzie argues.

"Yeah, sure. You just don't believe anyone who wrongs you deserves a second chance. A guy kidnaps me and drugs me? Sure, he deserves a second chance. Someone cheats on you? Nope. No second chance for the guy. Hyp-O-Crite."

Suzie growls, and I have to hold back a giggle. She sounds like a disgruntled puppy. I want to pat her head, but I know this puppy has all her teeth and isn't afraid to bite.

The saleswoman joins us, her arms piled high with wedding dresses. She places the dresses on a hanging rack as she introduces herself. "I'm Darra. I'll be helping you find the perfect dress today."

She motions Hailey over. Hailey gets to her feet and trudges to the rack.

"You're acting like you're going to an execution. You should be excited about getting married to the man you've loved since you were a pimple-faced teenager." Suzie giggles. "You should have seen her as a teenager. Talk about the ugly duckling transforming into a beautiful swan."

Hailey ignores Suzie, which is pretty much her go-to mode for dealing with her best friend. "I have no idea how to do all of this." She motions to the showroom with her arm. "Look at me. I have no idea how to look beautiful."

I roll my eyes. "Are you serious? You're gorgeous. With your body type, finding a dress should be easy."

Darra nods in agreement but before she can start a sales pitch, however, Hailey rushes to me and grabs my hands. "Can you help? Can you show me what dress will look good on me?"

"Did you ask me to be a bridesmaid because of my fashion sense?"

Her cheeks pink. "No, but it doesn't hurt."

I motion to the saleswoman. "I'm sure she can help you. She's an expert after all."

Hailey squeezes my hands. "But I want your help."

I sigh and get to my feet. "Fine. Let's have a look at these dresses."

She trails behind me as I go through the rack of dresses. "No. Yes. Definitely no. Yes. Are you kidding me? No. Worth a try. Yes." I quickly divide the dresses. "Here," I tell Darra as I hand her several dresses. "These are absolute no's." She takes the dresses and leaves.

Hailey stares at me with her mouth hanging open. "How did you do that? I thought I was going to have to try on two gazillion dresses."

"Do they have food?" Suzie guzzles a glass of champagne. "The bubbly is good, but if you're trying on two gazillion dresses, I'm going to need food."

"She's not trying on two gazillion dresses. You should never try on more than ten dresses. Otherwise, you'll be all confused and unable to make up your mind."

Hailey sticks her bottom lip out and pouts. "But how do I know which dresses to try on?"

"Easy. You're thin and tall. A textured and thicker fabric will create a fuller figure. Also, a closed neckline is more suitable."

Hailey gapes at me. "I don't know what most of those words mean. I mean I know what they mean individually, but put them together?" She shrugs.

Darra returns with another load of gowns. "You're going to stay this size, aren't you?"

Oh wow. How rude. Hailey doesn't seem bothered, though. She laughs. "I've been this size since eleventh grade. I don't think I'll be changing anytime soon." She leans forward and whispers to Darra like she has a secret. "And I eat whatever I want. Hamburgers, fries, cheese. You name it. I eat tons of food."

Darra's eyes widen as she takes a step back. "I didn't mean to offend."

Suzie snorts. "Sure, you did." She looks the sales assistant up and down. "I get it. You're jealous. Trust me, I understand." She motions to her body with her hand. Suzie is short but she's got curves for days. She looks like a pixie with her red spiky hair and short stature compared to Hailey's long, lean dancer body.

Darra's face is bright red, but she carries on. "Here's a dress I thought you might like."

Hailey takes the dress and immediately searches for the price tag. Her eyes widen when she finds it. "No way. I am not trying on a dress I can't afford. What if I love it? I still can't afford it."

"I'm sure we can arrange a discount."

Hailey hands the dress back. "No. I read all about avoiding steep discounts in wedding dresses."

"What did you do?" Suzie asks. "Research how to buy a wedding dress?"

"Of course, I did. I've never bought one before. I have no idea what I'm doing."

"What's your budget?" I ask as I walk over to the rack of dresses.

"Two-thousand."

Huh. I expected her to say a few hundred dollars. "Not a small budget then?"

A light shade of pink dusts her cheeks. "I've been saving for a while."

"She wants her dream wedding with her dream man," Suzie teases before putting her finger in her mouth and pretending to gag.

I ignore Suzie to study the rack of dresses. I find what I'm looking for with the third dress. I check the price to make sure it fits the budget before taking it off the rack.

"Here." I shove the dress in Hailey's hands. "This is the dress."

Hailey drags her feet as she follows Darra to the changing room.

I take a seat on the sofa to wait. Suzie skips over. She flops down on the sofa and nearly bounces right off.

"How many glasses of champagne have you had?"

She burps. "Not enough. Is there any alcohol in bubbly?"

I giggle. Oh, there is definitely alcohol in bubbly, and it will give you a killer headache if you over-indulge. I quickly learned to sip the stuff when I was a teenager and glasses were constantly being forced in my hand at family events. If you're wealthy, things like laws about legal drinking age don't exist.

"I'm going to find a bridesmaid gown." Suzie wobbles as she gets to her feet. I reach out to steady her, but she bats my hand away. "I'm fine."

Whatever. I lean back and take a sip of my champagne. It's not the good stuff, but I don't expect a wedding boutique in the mall to serve Bollinger. Oh wow. Rich girl Phoebe is still alive and kicking and apparently renting a room in my head. *Shut up*, I tell her. *We don't need $400 bottles of champagne.*

Hailey walks out of the dressing area and I gasp. "It's perfect."

The ivory wedding gown is strapless with a high bateau neckline and classic A-line dress with structured pleats. Hailey twirls around. Oh my. Aiden is going to love this. The dress is backless with a detachable train. The train flows outward with covered buttons and crystal trim detail.

I stand and approach her. She looks unsure. "If you don't buy that dress, I'm going to be extremely upset. It was made for you."

"Okay." She takes a deep breath. "I guess I found a wedding gown." She looks around. "Where's Suzie?"

Suzie bounces out of the dressing room. She's wearing a pink dress with ruffles everywhere. Seriously, they are everywhere – at the cuffs, the neckline, and around her waist. Those ruffles are every-darn-where. She twirls around. "What do you think?"

"I think you look like a stick of cotton candy." And cotton candy looks as unappetizing as it is sticky.

"I know. Isn't it awesome?"

She stops twirling around when she notices Hailey. "Holy moly. It's perfect." She runs forward and trips over the long hemline of her dress. She falls to the floor and rolls to her back. "I'm fine."

"We know!" Hailey and I shout in unison.

Suzie struggles to her feet. The champagne is affecting her more than she let on. She tucks the hem of the dress into the back of her underwear and walks around Hailey to study her dress.

"Holy cow! Aiden is going to kidnap you when he sees the dress is backless."

"Is it too much?"

"Are you crazy? It's perfect. Now, go buy it. We need to get out of here before we get kicked out."

I tilt my head toward Suzie who's now dancing around the place singing *Girls Just Want To Have Fun.* Of course, she has to touch every single dress she passes. The clerk is rushing around after her with her arms out as if she's expecting Suzie to fall at any minute now. And a fall is inevitable when we're talking about Suzie.

"And maybe we can go out the back way to get away from you know who."

"Not happening." Hailey dismisses my suggestion and holds out her hand to Suzie who rushes to her. "Come on, crazy girl, time to get dressed."

I grin as I watch them. Who knew escaping my life would lead me to having two close friends, one of whom is actually sane? Now if I could only get rid of one very annoying bounty hunter all would be right in my world.

Chapter 24

When in doubt, a breadstick makes a good gag. ~ Phoebe's rules for becoming a better person

"I don't know why we couldn't have snuck out the back," I grumble as we walk through the mall toward the food court.

"I'm not letting you get kidnapped on my watch," Suzie declares.

"Too late. Been there. Done that."

Hailey wraps her arm around me. "When the joking starts, the healing begins."

"Guru Hailey. Who knew?"

We walk into the pizzeria and take a booth in the back. Ryker follows us and settles at a table nearby.

Suzie frowns at him. "Aren't we going to ask him to sit with us?"

"No. We are not eating with him. Have you lost your mind?"

She tilts her head and studies the traitor. "He looks hungry."

"He can take care of himself."

The waitress approaches our table. "Can we get a big glass of water for her?"

Suzie pouts. "I thought we were drinking since we have a designated driver?"

I grab my head and rock back and forth in my seat to stop myself from launching over the table. I have never wanted to hurt someone in my life, but I'm sorely tempted to grab Suzie by the neck and shake her right now.

"It's not worth the jail time. Pretty girl like you would be eaten alive in prison."

I have to agree with Hailey. I may have toughened up from my rich girl lifestyle, but prison is not the place for me. I've had enough of sharing bathrooms with criminals to last me a lifetime.

The waitress returns with three glasses of water. Suzie grabs hers and drinks it down in one gulp. Most of the water lands on her top, but she acts like nothing happened.

"We'll have a large sausage and pepperoni pizza and a pitcher of whatever you have on tap."

The waitress nods and leaves.

"Aw! Stop kicking me," Hailey shouts before reaching down to rub her shin.

"Why is Suzie kicking you?"

"Um." Hailey bites her lip.

Geez. What now? "Out with it."

Hailey wrings her hands. "Well, Suzie and I were talking, and we think you should give Ryker a second chance."

I stick my finger in my ear and pretend to clear it. Surely, I'm hearing things. "I know Suzie here lives in crazy town, but you?"

She shrugs. "You have to admit anyone who's willing to take on the uncles is brave."

"Or stupid."

"Or maybe in love."

I bark out a laugh at Suzie's words. "You can't be serious. You don't kidnap someone you love." And if you do, I want nothing to do with your kinky games.

"How much of a smooth operator is your husband?"

My jaw clenches. When are people going to stop calling Theodore my husband? I know he's technically my husband, but he isn't who I choose to marry. And I left him, which makes him my ex.

Hailey holds her hands up. "Sorry. Sorry. Theodore. How much of a smooth operator is Theodore?"

I don't want to answer. No one has ever believed me before when I talked about Theodore's sleazy ways. But these two women who are doing a fine job of making me lose control of my temper are supposed to be my friends. Maybe they will believe me? I take a deep breath and take a chance.

"Theodore is a total fake. He has everyone convinced he's this caring, loving person, but he's about as caring as a dead fish and the only thing he loves is cold, hard cash. He doesn't give to charity because he cares about any of the causes. No. Giving to charity is all part of his image. And he certainly doesn't care about me or anyone else. Well, except for how he can use us to gain more wealth. When will he have enough money? He can't spend what he has in his lifetime anyway."

I didn't mean to rant, but it feels good to be able to talk about Theodore without worrying someone's going to report back to him. In my previous life, all my so-called friends were on his side. They thought I was deranged, and poor Theodore had to deal with his wife who didn't live in a reality. Yeah, right. I'll show you someone who doesn't live in reality. One clue. His name is Theodore.

"Then, it's entirely possible someone could believe Theodore when he tells them you're a spoiled little rich girl?"

I snarl at Hailey. "Don't you dare take Ryker's side. Ryker didn't take Theodore at his word. He met me. He took me out on a date, and he *kissed me!*"

"About this kiss." Suzie taps her fingers on the table. "On a scale of one to ten, with ten being instant orgasm and one being slimy fish, how does Ryker rate?" She sighs as she places her elbows on the table and cups her chin in her hands. "The idea that fine piece of man flesh doesn't know how to kiss hurts."

I grunt. "He knows how to kiss."

The man knows entirely too well how to kiss. His lips are soft, such a contradiction of the hard man himself. And his tongue? It performs acrobatics I didn't know tongues could perform. I get goosebumps merely thinking about his lips on mine.

Suzie points at me and her finger circles my face. "That mushy look you're currently sporting is why I want you to give him a second chance."

I snap my teeth at her finger. She is making me crazy. I don't snap my teeth at people. Or the old Phoebe didn't. Maybe the new Phoebe does snap her teeth. I narrow my eyes at her. She winks in return, completely uncaring I tried to bite her finger off.

"Isn't it my choice to give someone a second chance?"

"If someone knows about needing a second chance, it should be you."

That's it. I'm taking Suzie down. How dare she? Ms. Won't Give A Cheater A Second Chance. I lunge across the table.

Hailey pulls me back. "You should at least talk to him. There's a reason the uncles trust him with your safety, after all."

This is news to me. "They do?"

"Yeah. They had a big powwow at the pub. Apparently, Ryker laid it all on the line and they agreed he could protect you."

"How do you know all this?"

"Aiden told me."

"What else did he tell you?"

She frowns. "Nothing. He wouldn't tell me why the uncles are giving Ryker a second chance. And trust me, I did everything I could think of to get the information."

Suzie leans forward. "Oh yeah? Tell us everything. All the deets."

Hailey blushes. "No."

Suzie wiggles her brows. "Oh, come on. At least tell us about his schlong."

"I am not talking to you about my future husband's penis."

"Penis sounds clinical. At least use the word dick. Or cock. Yeah, cock is better."

"Fine!" I throw my arms in the air. I will literally do anything if Suzie will stop saying the word cock in a crowded restaurant.

"I'll talk to him." Suzie claps and I point at her. "I'm not saying I'll give him a second chance, but I'll talk to him."

I'm sure I'm making the biggest mistake of my life – my marriage included – but I'm a big girl, I can handle talking to the man who crushed my heart. I'm sure I can find some big girl panties in the pile of stuff the uncles dumped in Pops' apartment. All I need is a pair of big girl panties and I'm all set.

Chapter 25

Always make sure your big girl panties are firmly secured. ~ Phoebe's rules for becoming a better person

"CAN WE GO SOMEWHERE else to talk?" Ryker asks as he looks around McGraw's Pub at the uncles who are sitting in their corner booth making no attempt to hide the fact they're listening.

"I said I would talk to you. I didn't say I'd talk to you alone." I lean forward and hiss in his face. "Because, in case you forgot, the last time we were alone, you kidnapped me."

The uncles cheer from their corner. I roll my eyes at them. What are they cheering for? They were the ones who wanted me to give Ryker a second chance in the first place. And no, I'm not giving him a second chance. I'm giving him a chance to explain because claiming he thought I was a spoiled rich girl is not an explanation.

"Okay." Ryker gives in.

Um, what? I was gearing up for a fight. I'm not used to men agreeing with me. The men in my life roll right on over me.

No, the men in my *former life* rolled over me. This Phoebe does not get treated like a doormat.

I wait for him to start explaining why we're here, but he doesn't speak. He looks happy to sit across from me and gawk at me all night long. Not happening.

"What did you want to talk about?"

He rubs a hand over his face. "I want to apologize."

Before I can respond, the men in the cheap seats start yelling. "Accept his apology!"

Enough! I've had it. I jump to my feet and stomp my way to the uncles. I slam my hands down on the table and lean forward to glare at them.

"Stop it! Stop acting like you care about me. You proved you don't give the first damn about me when you forced me to listen to my kidnapper days after the kidnapping."

"Now, Doll—"

I cut Lenny off with a swoosh of my hand. "No. I don't want to hear it."

Wally stands and puts his hands on my shoulders. "We were wrong, and we're sorry."

My eyes widen. They're apologizing for being traitors?

"We wanted you to have the full story of what Theodore was capable of, but we went about it the wrong way."

They're admitting to a mistake in addition to an apology? This can't be true. I raise my hand to check his temperature. "Are you feeling okay?"

"I'm fine, and before you ask, I haven't been abducted by aliens either."

I shrug. "Alien abduction does seem to be going around."

"Told you!" Barney shouts. "Aliens are real."

A smile starts to spread over my face before I can stop it.

"She smiled! We're off the hook!"

I giggle and take a step back out of Wally's arms right into a brick wall. Only this brick wall smells like heaven. Ryker. "What are you doing?"

"I'm protecting you. I'm not going to let anyone hurt you again. Not even your uncles."

"You're not my protector."

He smirks. "Sure, I am." I shake my head. "Come on, Princess." He reaches out for my hand. "We have a lot to discuss."

"You better treat her right," Lenny orders.

Quick as can be, Ryker shoves me behind him. "No, *you* better treat her right." He growls. "I admit I screwed up, royally, but I was only getting to know my princess. She trusted you guys, thought you were her family. You're not giving her the choice of whether or not to talk to me was a bigger betrayal."

Sid smirks. "But you wouldn't have been able to talk to her without us."

"Man, pay attention. I would have kept trying. With or without your help." He spins around. I can see the determination in his eyes when he looks down at me. "And I will keep trying, Princess. Until you accept my apology and we can start over."

"Start over?" Shit. My question came out all squeaky. I clear my voice. "Start over?"

He grabs my hand and pulls me back to our table. He helps me into my seat before sitting down across from me.

"I'm sorry. I want a second chance. I realize I screwed up big time. But the way I felt for you scared me shitless."

Geez. Are we in a romance novel? How effing cliché. "Come on, you can do better than that."

"You're married and your husband hired me to watch over you and here I was kissing you and having all kinds of feelings for you. I don't mix business and pleasure. But one look at you and all my rules flew out the window."

There's one problem with what's he saying. "I'm not married."

"Honey, you are." I hiss. "I know you don't want to be. Trust me, after investigating your asshat of a husband, I understand. But you're not divorced yet."

"But his wife, Phoebe Abbot, is dead. He's a widower. Phoebe Adams is not married."

"Okay." He nods. "I'll concede Phoebe Adams is not married. But you weren't Phoebe Adams to me before. You were Phoebe Abbot."

"A target," I hiss.

Ryker's eyes flash with pain and he flinches. "I'm sorry. Fuck. You will never know how sorry I am. But I couldn't do it. I couldn't take you back to him."

Couldn't take me back to him? Has he suffered from brain damage causing amnesia? "Don't lie to me. We were in a motel on a highway on our way to California. You were taking me back to him."

"No, I wasn't."

I grab my coat and get to my feet. "This is a waste of time. Your lying to me will get you nowhere."

He grabs my hand to stop me. His thumb smooths over my inner wrist and my body warms and my stomach flip flops. Why does one simple, innocent touch from him feel better than anything I've felt from a man before? It's not right. He betrayed me.

"Please. Let me explain."

I tug my hand away and plop down. "Explain. Explain how we weren't on the way to California."

"Did you not look at where we were?"

Is he serious? "Um, no. Strange as it may seem I didn't pay attention to what direction we were traveling in when I was drugged out of my mind."

"Shit. I'm sorry." He runs a hand through his hair and pulls on the ends. "I knew Theodore hired at least one other bounty hunter to find you. I needed to make our escape look real."

"Our escape? You have a funny way of describing a kidnapping. And funny as in strange, not funny as in haha."

He ignores me and finally explains. "I wasn't taking you back to Theodore. Even before I learned about the baby issue, I knew something was wrong with the situation."

"We'll get back to the part about you not taking me to Theodore in a minute. First, I want to know why you didn't say anything?"

"I should have. I realize my mistake now. I should have told the uncles and got them on my side."

"Here! Here!" the uncles shout from the other side of the room. I ignore them.

"Prove it. Prove you weren't taking me back to Theodore." Because Phoebe 2.0 is no naïve fool who believes everything a man tells her. No, she needs cold, hard facts. I kind of like Phoebe 2.0. Phoebe 1.0 should have gotten an upgrade much sooner.

"We weren't on our way to California. Ask the uncles. We were on 1-94 on our way to Montana. If we had been heading for California, I would have taken I-80 to Omaha."

I look over at the uncles who nod their heads. "Okay, say I believe we were going to Montana, why Montana?"

"I have a place there no one knows about. I planned to hide you there until I could figure out what to do."

I raise my hand to indicate he should stop. "Wait. Hold up. You were going to hide me? Until what? Theodore got tired of looking for me?"

He shrugs. "I admit I didn't have much a plan, but I needed to move you. I could feel the other bounty hunter getting close, and then Theodore called and demanded I take you. I didn't have time to put together a plan."

"Why?"

He raises an eyebrow. "Why what?"

"Why would you risk your job for me? And why not tell me? Why drug me?"

"I didn't know how close the other bounty hunter was. And I'm pretty sure Theodore has eyes on me. I needed to make it look real until I could get you to Montana."

"But why risk your job at all?"

He chuckles. "You don't get it." Obviously not. "I'm falling for you, Princess. You think you were the only one affected by our kiss? You'd be wrong."

He reaches out and grabs my hands. "Please. Give me another chance. I promise not to lie to you ever again."

"Even if it's for my own good?"

"Even if it's for your own good." He clears his throat. "I know I'm not good enough for you, but I'm not giving you up."

I must be crazy because I'm actually considering giving the man who kidnapped me a second chance. But he didn't kidnap me to drag me back to California. He kidnapped me to save me from California and Theodore and all the things Theodore would do to me.

I may be a fool for giving Ryker a second chance, but I'd be a bigger fool to ignore how the man makes me feel. I've read enough romance novels to know I shouldn't let an opportunity to explore the chemistry between us slip away.

I close my eyes and take a deep breath. Phoebe 2.0 can do this. She can take a chance. After all, she's survived having her heart broken before. She can do it again if necessary.

"Okay. Let's start over." I pull my hands away from his and wave. "Hi, I'm Phoebe. What's your name?"

A smile stretches from ear to ear over his face and his mossy green eyes twinkle. Where do I sign up for trouble? Because this bad boy has trouble stamped all over him.

Chapter 26

A lady never reveals her secrets, but I'm no lady.
~ Phoebe's rules for becoming a better person

"Oh, look, someone's allowed inside the office today. What's changed?" Suzie wiggles her eyebrows.

I don't bother responding to her. No doubt she has already heard from the uncles and Pops about last night. Those men gossip worse than old ladies.

"Ignore her," I tell Ryker who has followed me to the office.

Ryker was waiting for me when I walked out of the apartment above McGraw's Pub this morning. He didn't say a word, merely opened the passenger door to his truck, and waited for me to make my own decision.

Since it's freezing outside with the wind whipping off the lake, it was an easy decision to make. It had nothing to do with how sexy the man looked in his ripped jeans and long-sleeved t-shirt stretched over the muscles of his chest. Nothing at all.

Lola comes barreling out of Hailey's office. Her hind legs slide out from under her as she takes the corner, but she doesn't slow down. She jumps up on me and starts loving on me.

"Down!" At Ryker's command, Lola drops into a sitting position. "Basket." He points in the direction of Hailey's office.

Lola whines once and then trots away.

I gape at the big bad bounty hunter with my mouth hanging open.

"What can I say? Dogs love me."

I laugh at his use of my words against me.

Suzie raises her hand. "I vote he can stay."

"Too bad klutzy girls don't get votes."

"I'm not a klutz," she mumbles, but I've seen the proof. I know the truth.

Hailey walks out of her office with her hair a mess and her lips swollen. Aiden swaggers out behind her with a smirk on his face.

I raise an eyebrow at Suzie. "You didn't stop them?"

"I'm not a cockblocker."

Aiden snorts. "Sure, you aren't." He kisses Hailey on the forehead, does a chin lift in Ryker's direction, and takes off.

Suzie crosses her arms over her chest. "If this office is becoming the love shack, I'm not sure I want to work here anymore."

Hailey rumples her hair. "You're the one who pushed us together. You reap what you sow."

"What's on the agenda for today?" Ryker is obviously done listening to our joking around.

"Well, we were going to talk about you and Pheebs all day, but now you've gone and ruined all our fun." Suzie pouts.

"I told you not to call me Pheebs."

"Sorry. Not sorry. Phoebe is a stuck-up bitch. Since you're no longer a stuck-up bitch, I've hereby renamed you Pheebs."

I have no words. Luckily, Hailey does. "I need your help with an insurance case if you're up for it."

Why wouldn't I be up for it? "Sure, let's go."

Suzie claps. "And I get to play with Lola all day."

"And do the accounts." Hailey reminds her.

"Yeah, yeah, whatever." She's already on the floor calling Lola to her.

When we reach the company SUV, Hailey frowns at Ryker. "Are you coming with us?"

"I'll follow you." He tilts his head in the direction of his truck parked a few spots away.

"What's the deal with the insurance claim?" I ask as soon as we're settled in the car.

Hailey giggles. "I get it. You don't want to talk about whatever's going on with you and Ryker. No worries. I won't pry. But if you ever need to talk, I'm here."

"Thanks."

As we drive to the suspect's house, she fills me in on the case. Douglas Flint was working as a car mechanic at one of the local car dealerships when part of a ramp swung around and hit his ankle. He's now suing the dealership as he can no longer fulfill his function since he can't be on his feet all day and walking is torture for him.

"If this is true, I feel sorry for the guy. I broke my foot once when I fell off a swing. It was agony."

"You were allowed to play in an actual playground?"

As if. "Not an actual playground. We had our own in the backyard. I was generously allowed to play there until I was ten. Then, the playground was packed up and my mother put in a rose garden." A rose garden she never visited as far as I know.

Hailey pulls over and parks. She points to a house three doors down. "Flint's place is there."

I grab the camera case and pull out the camera and start fiddling with it. "I hope we don't have to sit here all day."

"I warned you being a PI is boring."

She did, but I didn't listen. Why would I? I'd found two women who were willing to be my friends despite knowing nothing about my past and my family. In my experience, people couldn't wait to be friends with me fast enough once they learned my last name. But Hailey and Suzie didn't know my real last name. They were willing to take a chance on me anyway. Of course, I couldn't sign up to work with them fast enough.

Hailey sits up in her seat. "The garage door's opening." She switches on the car.

A muscle car backs out of the drive and takes off down the street. We follow. I look in the side mirror and see Ryker's truck is behind us as well. Yippee, it's a convoy.

Douglas Flint drives to the nearest Wal-Mart and parks in a handicapped spot. He grabs a cart and throws his cane in it. He limps as he walks into the store.

"Damn. His injury looks serious," Hailey says as I snap away. "Can you follow him?"

I nod and jump out. I hurry to catch up to Flint as he disappears into the store. I hear a vehicle screech to a halt and a door slam, but my attention is riveted on my target as I rush inside.

Flint scurries through the store to the electronics department. For someone with an injury, he sure moves fast. I nearly have to run to keep up and I have long legs.

I watch as he fills his cart with ink cartridges. What the heck is he printing? No one needs that much ink. He leaves the department to walk to the checkout. I pass Ryker as I follow Flint. I wave and he shakes his head at me. What? It's rude not to greet people you know.

Flint motors straight past the checkout and heads for the door. What in the world? Is he stealing an entire cart full of ink cartridges? I keep my camera at waist height so it's not obvious what I'm up to and I snap a few pictures of him rushing out of the store to his car.

He dumps the cartridges in his trunk, leaves the cart where it is, and jumps behind the wheel. A car squeals to a halt next to me and the door flies open. "Get in!" Hailey orders. I barely manage to close the door before she takes off after Flint.

"Did he seriously walk out of there without paying?"

"Sure did. He breezed out of there like he owned the place. No one bothered to look at him twice. But what is he going to do with a trunk load of ink cartridges?"

"I bet he's planning on selling them on eBay. Ink cartridges average about thirty bucks a pop."

"And he had at least fifty of them in his cart." I quickly calculate in my head. "That's fifteen-hundred-dollars for an hour's work."

"Work?" Hailey frowns. "Since when is stealing work?"

"You know what I mean."

She turns right to follow Flint. "This isn't the way to his house."

"Don't tell me he's going to rob another store."

We drive for twenty minutes until we reach another Wal-Mart. "Holy moly. He is going to rob another store."

"Not being able to be on his feet all day isn't slowing him down at all," I say as we drive into the parking lot. "Should I inform Wal-Mart?"

"I'll call Aiden. I'm sure the insurance company would love a bunch of footage of him being a thief, but I'm not going to sit here and watch some guy rob store after store." She reaches for her phone.

I open the door to follow Flint, but Ryker blocks me. Where did he come from?

"This store is packed. I can't protect you."

I huff. "I'm trying to do my job."

He nods toward Hailey. "She's calling Aiden, isn't she?"

I deflate. There's no reason for me to follow Douglas if the man is going to end up in cuffs soon anyway.

"Get back in the car and wait for back up."

Hailey's hanging up as I get back in the passenger seat.

"Ryker pull the big bad protector card on you?"

I grunt. Obviously.

"Don't worry. Once the police arrest Douglas Flint, we'll still get our payday."

The police arrive and park at the front of the store. Hailey and I get out and walk to them. The driver rolls down the window. "You Aiden's woman?"

Hailey rolls her eyes. "I'm Hailey. We can point out Douglas Flint when he exits."

I hope he has a cart of ink cartridges with him. Otherwise, we're going to look like fools. We wait two minutes for Flint to walk out. He doesn't make us look like fools. His cart is stuffed with ink cartridges.

The officers exit their squad car and meander toward him. As soon as Flint sees the officers, he shoves the cart at them and takes off running.

"Broken foot, my ass," Hailey mumbles as I lift the camera and take pictures. "And you were worried about getting the money shot."

She throws her arm around me. "You should learn to trust me."

We watch as the officers tackle Flint to the ground and cuff him before hauling him to his feet.

"Welp. Our work here is done." She looks over to Ryker's truck. "Yep. We better leave before someone has a brain hemorrhage."

I glance over. Ryker's hands are gripping the steering wheel and his jaw is clenched. I bet he's grinding his teeth as well.

"Someone needs to take a chill pill," I mutter but follow her back to our SUV.

"If you wanted a chill man, you shouldn't have fallen for a bounty hunter."

Fallen for a bounty hunter? I haven't fallen for anyone. Except the words feel like a lie. Shit. Am I falling for Ryker?

Chapter 27

If all else fails, kick him in the balls. ~ Phoebe's
rules for becoming a better person

I WALK OUT OF McGraw's Pub the next morning with a spring in my step. I spent most of yesterday evening chatting with Ryker and getting to know the man behind the gruff bounty hunter. Talking over the phone instead of in-person helped me to open up about the emotional abuse I suffered under Theodore. I talked about things I never thought I'd tell another living being.

Ryker opened up about his past as well. He isn't from California after all. He's from Montana, which is why he keeps a cabin there. He told me a bit about growing up in the foster care system. I knew there were problems with the system, but I didn't realize how bad it truly is.

I wave as Ryker's truck rounds the corner. An engine revs and I watch as a car comes out of nowhere to screech to a halt right in front of him. He slams on his brakes with barely enough time to stop his truck before it barrels into the car.

What the hell? I start running in his direction to check if he's okay. *Please be okay.*

Ryker opens his door. "Run, Phoebe. Run!"

Run? I'm not questioning him. If he says run, I'll run. I make a U-turn and sprint back to McGraw's. Pops is inside and I know for a fact he keeps a shotgun under the bar.

I have one hand on the door when someone yanks me back. "Phoebe dearest, you didn't think you could run away from me, did you?"

I snarl. I absolutely loathe this man. Theodore Abbot, the man who put the ass into asshole. I snatch my arm away and turn to face him.

"I'm not going anywhere with you."

"Tut. Tut. You act like you have a choice."

I get right up in his face. "I do have a choice, asshole."

The fake smile drops from his face and the snake beneath is revealed. His nose flares as his eyes fill with venom. "Don't force me to make you."

"Fuck. You," I tell him and then spit in his face. "I'm not going anywhere with you."

"My. My. We have a lot of corrections to perform when we get home."

Once upon a time, his words would have caused fear to run through my veins. No more. Now I know I can get away from him and make a life without him. A life I'm not willing to give up.

I push him away and reach around to open the door to the pub. He grabs the collar of my coat and drags me toward the black BMW waiting in the street. I struggle with him but he's stronger than I gave him credit for. I unzip my coat and slip out of it. Once I'm free, I rush to the door.

Theodore catches me before I can reach it. He grabs me by the hair and tugs me back to the car. I claw at his hands and arms, but his grip doesn't falter. I can feel the blood oozing out of his skin, but his grip remains steady.

I try to remember the lessons from my self-defense class, but no one talked about how to get away from an assailant grabbing your hair. I do remember one lesson, though. *If all else fails, kick him in the nuts.* I swing my leg back and connect with some part of Theodore.

He swings me around by my hair. "Remember you made me do this." He pulls his right hand back and clocks me in the jaw. The hit stuns me and I drop my hands. He takes advantage of my momentary disorientation and throws me into the rear seat of the car like I'm a ragdoll.

The driver takes off with a squeal of the tires. I look out the rear window when I hear the unmistakable sound of metal on metal. Ryker is in his truck pushing the car blocking him out of his way.

A spark of hope ignites. Ryker will save me.

Theodore chuckles but the sound is devoid of humor. "Don't worry, my dear. I'll have your boyfriend taken care of." He growls. "He better not have gotten you pregnant."

He can't seriously take care of Ryker, can he? What about the uncles? Maybe they'll help.

"And as for those ex-Army losers you hang about with, don't count on them coming after you anytime soon either. They'll be entirely too busy."

"What did you do?" I wouldn't put anything past him.

He smiles and it looks downright wicked. How can other people not see what an evil man he is?

"Since you'll never see those lowlifes again, I'll satisfy your curiosity." He doesn't elaborate. Instead, he takes his time unwinding his scarf from his neck and placing it on his lap.

I nearly roll my eyes at his old tricks. He gets off on making me wait. If I get impatient and ask, he makes me wait longer. Guess what? I'm done with his bullshit.

"What did you do?"

He hums and looks out the window. I grab his scarf and throw it on the floor. Childish I know, but it bugs the hell out of him.

"Careful. I'm not afraid of hitting you again."

My jaw aches from where he clocked me and my scalp burns from where he pulled my hair, but I refuse to let him see my pain. "Go ahead. See if I care." I'm taunting him and it feels good. It feels good not to be cowered by him.

"I'm afraid one of their houses caught on fire." He feigns a gasp as he places a hand over his heart. "What a shame."

I swallow my laugh before I remember I'm done hiding my emotions from this man. I chuckle and shake my head as if I haven't a care in the world. "And you think they won't catch on to the fire being a diversion?"

My uncles – the men who invaded a hotel room to save me – would never fall for an obvious trick.

"Oh, they not only fell for it. There may have been some injuries while they were putting out the fire. In fact, I believe one of the old men is in the hospital now."

The blood in my veins turns to ice. And I thought I couldn't hate this man anymore than I already do. "Who's injured? Who's in the hospital?"

He shrugs. "It's of no concern."

Of no concern? "They are human beings, not pawns in your game."

"Funny. I'm pretty sure they are pawns."

The man has no problem admitting to arson and injuring people. Pure evil. But no one ever believes me when I tell them about the things he says and does. But hold on. If presented with cold hard evidence, they'd have to believe me. And there's a simple way for me to collect the evidence. I have a recorder in my bag. The perks of being a PI. I always carry a camera and a recorder with me now.

While I search my bag, I need to keep him distracted, which is easy enough. He loves to brag.

"How did you know I wasn't dead?"

He chuckles and this time there's real humor in the sound. "I know better than to believe that bounty hunter person would let you go. He's obviously fallen under your spell. Although I'm not sure how you managed to fool him into thinking you care for him. You never were good at playacting."

I do care for Ryker, but he doesn't need to know the truth. He'll only use the knowledge to hurt me somehow.

"But there was a death certificate."

"Without a body?" He shakes his head. "I'm not a fool."

I grapple for another subject. "What are you going to do with me?"

His grin is wide. "I'm going to take you home and impregnate you." He makes it sound soooo romantic.

"What if I don't want to be impregnated?"

"My dear, it's adorable you think you have a choice."

"You can't force me to have sex with you."

He places his hand over his mouth as he yawns. "If you don't want to give me what I want, I won't give you what you need."

I'm afraid to ask, but I do anyway because I've found the recorder and managed to switch it on. "What do you mean?"

He sighs. "Don't be silly. You know exactly what I mean. I'll keep you locked up in your room. Only this time there won't be any food or water. And there certainly won't be any access to the internet or your phone."

"But if I have sex with you, you'll let me eat?" He nods. "That's rape."

"Potato, potahto."

With the recorder running, I want to have him confess to as many illegal deeds as possible. No matter where I end up, I'll be able to use this tape against him somehow. I refuse to believe this is the end for me. I've come too far to return to my gilded cage in California.

"You didn't have to set fire to one of the uncle's houses, you know."

His nose turns down in disgust. "My dear, you know I never do any dirty work myself. Now, I'm done talking. Time for you to take a nap."

I open my mouth to tell him I have no intention of taking a nap but halt when I notice he's holding a syringe. I drop the recorder in my bag and lift my hands to fight him off.

I kick out and he grabs my leg. "This is a good a place as any," he says before injecting me in my calf.

Chapter 28

If you see a chance, take it by the balls and run with it. ~ Phoebe's rules for becoming a better person

"Get us out of this city," Theodore orders.

Theodore? What? Am I having a nightmare? I try to open my eyes, but they're glued shut. Cars honk and there's a squeal of brakes. Shit. It all comes back to me. Theodore dragging me into his car. Ryker unable to get to me. The uncles not— Oh no. One of the uncles is hurt.

I can't let thoughts of the uncles and Ryker distract me. I need to get myself out of this situation. Step one. Find out where the heck I am. I force one eye open and look outside. Huh. We're still in Milwaukee? I must not have been out long. The material of my jeans and knee-high boots must have protected me from getting too much of the drug inside my body.

"Make sure the jet is fueled and prepared to take off."

At Theodore's words, my heart thumps loud enough I'm sure he'll hear and realize I'm awake. If he manages to get me on the jet, I'll be lost. There's no way Ryker or the uncles can follow me into the air.

I need to get out of here now. There is no time for being sneaky. I reach for the handle and curve my hand around it. As soon as the car slows, I'm making a break for it.

I keep one eye open and watch the street for a stoplight. The other eye, the one closest to Theodore, I keep closed. *Please, please, please, don't realize I'm awake.*

Theodore isn't paying any attention to me. Of course not. I'm merely a possession after all. A possession with entirely too much attitude. But still just a possession.

I notice a stoplight up ahead. The light is green but as I watch it switches to yellow and the cars in front of us slow. This is my chance. I take a deep breath and pull the handle. The door flies open and I nearly fall out of the car.

"Stop!" Theodore yells. "You'll only make it worse for yourself."

I ignore him and start running. I run across the street and look around. Where am I? I need to contact Ryker, but my phone is in the car.

The tires of the black BMW squeal as it makes a U-turn. It catches up to me and slams to a stop in front of me. *Shit.* I'm out of time. I run toward the convenience store on the corner. He won't forcibly take me from a store in front of witnesses, will he?

"Stop! Someone stop my wife! She's mentally ill and needs help."

Well, damn. I guess he will detain me against my will in front of witnesses. A truck screeches to a halt in front of me and Ryker jumps out.

"In the truck. Lock the doors," he yells and throws me the keys.

I raise my hands too late to catch them, but they fall to the ground. I drop to my knees and scoop them up. As soon as I'm back on my feet, I race toward his truck. My hands are unsteady, and my body is shaking. It takes me two tries to open the door and I slip trying to climb into the truck, but I eventually manage to haul myself into the vehicle. As soon as I'm in the seat, I slam the door closed behind me and hit the locks.

Ryker prowls toward Theodore and his driver who take one look at him and retreat. They get back into their car and it peels out. They don't get far. A blue sedan with a strobe light flashing halts in front of the car blocking them in. Aiden opens the door with his weapon pulled.

"Get out of the car with your arms raised."

The driver doesn't hesitate. As soon as he's out of the car, a uniformed officer approaches and grabs him by the upper arm. He spins him around and cuffs him before hauling him away from the scene.

I expect Theodore to refuse. He doesn't follow anyone's orders after all. But he too steps out of the car with his hands raised.

"Officer, this is a misunderstanding. I'm merely trying to get my wife home. She's mentally ill and needs treatment."

I growl and my hands curl into fists. I am not mentally ill! And I'm about done with him making ludicrous claims about me. I unlock the doors and jump out of Ryker's truck.

"I am not mentally ill! You're a sick bastard."

Theodore shakes his head with a frown on his face. "You see what I mean?"

"All I see is a woman who doesn't want to be with you who was detained against her will."

I don't hear any more as Ryker is there pushing me away from the scene.

"I'm not going anywhere." I yank on my arm, but his grip doesn't weaken.

"Princess, I just watched a man drag you by your hair, punch you, and then drug you. Please, don't fight me." Ryker looks me in the eyes, and I see anguish there. I give up fighting.

"I promise you'll get your day in court, but let Aiden arrest him first, yeah?"

I can hardly say no to the man who rescued me from the grips of Satan. I allow him to lift me into his truck. When I look back toward Aiden and Theodore, the action is over. Aiden has Theodore cuffed and in the back of his car. He slams the door before giving Ryker a chin lift.

Ryker buckles my seatbelt for me before shutting my door and walking around to the driver's seat.

"Where are we going?" I ask as he starts up the truck and heads in the opposite direction of Aiden's police cruiser.

"The hospital."

"The hospital? I don't need the hospital." Oh wait. The uncles! Is one of them hospitalized? "What happened to the uncles? Was someone hurt?"

He snickers. "They're fine. Pissed as hell they didn't get to take part in your rescue operation but fine."

What a relief. "Then, why are we going to the hospital?"

His jaw locks. "To have your injuries seen to."

I wave away his concern. "I'm fine."

"There's blood dripping from your hands and you were drugged."

I look at my hands. My nails are shredded. Good. I did some damage to Theodore's arms then. "This is nothing a manicure can't fix." I'm lying. A manicure can't fix this damage. My nails are going to be a mess for a while, but there's nothing a hospital can do about it.

"Your face," he growls.

I flip down the visor to look in the mirror. The right side of my jaw is purple and swollen. "I'm sure the police have an ice pack I can borrow," I say and flip the visor back up.

Ryker takes his eyes off the road for a second to glance in my direction. A vein in his forehead pulses when his eyes fall upon my jaw. I reach over and grab his hand before he can speak.

"I'm okay, Ryker. Nothing happened. Can we please go to the police station? I want to give my statement. I need to make sure that rat bastard gets locked up."

His hand spasms in mine before he agrees. "Okay, but the first sign you're not feeling well and I'm taking you to the hospital."

I nod. I won't be going to the hospital, but it doesn't hurt to let him believe I'm complacent.

When we walk into the police station fifteen minutes later, Hailey and Suzie are waiting for us. Hailey takes one look at my face and marches toward the door marked 'personnel only'. "I'm going to beat the shit out of your ex."

Ryker grabs her by her hoodie and pulls her back. "It's never a good idea to announce you're going to commit assault at the police station."

"Yeah," Suzie agrees. "Maybe we should poison him instead." She winks at me. "I got this. My chemistry skills are fantabulous." She drums her fingers together and wiggles her eyebrows. "Bwah-haha."

Aiden walks out from behind the personnel door. "Phoebe, are you ready to give your statement?"

"Where's Theodore? Have you got him locked up?"

His jaw clenches. "He's invoked his right to counsel and is waiting for his lawyer."

Of course, he has. Classic Theodore. Let someone else do the heavy lifting.

Aiden squeezes my shoulder. "Don't worry, sweetheart. There are tons of witnesses to your abduction. He won't get away with this."

He doesn't realize how slippery Theodore can be. The man can wiggle his way out of most any legal complication. Money talks, after all.

"You got this," Hailey says and grabs my hand. "You are not the scared woman who showed up in our offices months ago. No, you are Phoebe Adams, kick-ass PI."

Suzie grabs my other hand and squeezes. "And there's always the poison option."

Aiden raises his eyebrow, but Ryker shakes his head. "You don't want to know."

"Come on, let's get this done."

"We're not leaving her," Hailey declares.

"Yeah, this police station is totally cool. It's just like a movie set. I'm not going anywhere."

Aiden shakes his head before leading us deeper into the station.

Suzie vibrates in excitement. "This is a movie set," she whispers. "Do you think they'd mind if I take some pictures?"

Ryker grunts from behind me. Apparently, I have an entourage to give my statement. Take that, Theodore. You thought you cut me off from all my friends and family, but you didn't. No, this family – the one I created – will not desert me.

Aiden opens a door to what looks like an interrogation room. Before I can walk in, Ryker grabs my shoulder and stops me. He twirls me around. "You sure you're ready for this? Aiden can wait a day or two for you to give your statement."

I am so ready to get rid of my asshat husband it isn't funny. I roll up on my tiptoes and touch my lips to Ryker's. "Yeah, babe, I'm ready."

He searches my eyes. Apparently, he finds what he's looking for as he nods. Aiden slaps his back.

"Phoebe's got this. She's strong."

My heart warms at Aiden's words. No one's ever called me strong before. I totally do got this.

"Let's do this!" I announce and march into the room.

Chapter 29

Put on your big girl panties and take a chance once in a while. ~ Phoebe's rules for becoming a better person

LUNCHTIME HAS COME AND gone by the time we leave the police station. Theodore's legal counsel has arrived, but he's still refusing to answer any questions. Of course, he is. The man answers to no one. Or so he thinks. I hope being in a state where his influence is less than in California will help keep his ass in jail.

Thanks to my statement and other witness statements, Theodore has been charged with unlawful confinement, assault, criminal endangerment, and a whole slew of other charges.

Ryker lifts me into his truck. I stop him before he can shut the door. "What happens when he gets out on bail?"

"With these charges, I don't think he'll get bail."

How cute. He thinks Theodore will be denied bail. There's no way the man who calls himself my husband will be remanded to jail. But I'm not starting an argument with Ryker in the parking lot of a police station. "Say he does get bail. What then?"

"Bail will be at least a cool million. Theodore isn't going anywhere."

I grab his hand. "A million is nothing to a man like Theodore."

Ryker's eyes widen slightly before determination sets in. "We'll deal with it when it happens."

We drive to McGraw's where the uncles and Hailey and Suzie are waiting on us. Suzie and Hailey left while I was still answering a gazillion questions from Officer Kent. And by 'left' I mean Officer Kent 'requested' Suzie leave after she interrupted his questions for the fifth time to ask if she could see his badge and gun.

As soon as we enter the pub, I race to the uncles. Sid has a bandage over his forehead. "Oh no. You were hurt. I'm sorry."

Sid grunts. "Nothing for you to apologize for. You're not responsible for your ex-husband's actions."

"But you were hurt." I reach forward to touch the bandage, but he grabs my hand to stop me.

"The nurse insisted I get stitches, which I didn't need."

Barney chuckles. "You didn't look like you minded at the time. And Nurse Mary Ann gave you her number, didn't she?"

"I thought you had wife number six on the hook?"

"Number five," he corrects.

Barney leans forward and whisper-shouts, "Number six didn't work out."

Wally clears his throat. "Can we move on from the woman who stalked Sid now?" My eyes widen. Someone was stalking Sid?

"It's not stalking when I like it," Sid mumbles.

I giggle. Is he serious?

Lenny grabs my hand. "How are you, Doll?"

Ryker wraps an arm around my waist and pulls me close forcing Lenny to drop his hand. Lenny smirks and raises his hands in surrender. I roll my eyes.

"Overprotective much?"

His nose brushes against my hair before he whispers in my ear, "Need I remind you I watched you taken away from me this morning?"

I shiver at the sound of his deep, growly voice in my ear. The sound causes my nerve endings to wake up and say *Hello! Where have you been all my life?* Apparently, my nerve endings are cliché.

Pops joins us. "Sit. Sit. You need to eat."

My eyes widen when I see the plates of burgers and fries. "Um."

"I'm not taking no for an answer. Sit. Eat."

The uncles make room for us and Hailey and Suzie join us for a late lunch.

I barely finish my food before my eyes start to close of their own accord. The next thing I know I'm in Ryker's arms as he carries me across the pub toward the stairs to the apartment above.

"What are you doing? Don't you need to get to work?"

He snorts. "You're not getting rid of me that easy."

I bury my head in his chest to hide my smile. His body moves as he chuckles. I guess I'm not fooling him for one second.

He carries me up the stairs straight to the bedroom I'm currently using at Pops' place. He sets me on the bed before removing my shoes. He pulls back the covers and I scoot under them. I watch as he sits on the bed and removes his boots.

"What are you doing?"

"I'm not leaving you alone."

I should probably argue. Tell him it's too soon for him to be sleeping in bed next to me, but I'm selfish. I don't want him to go anywhere.

He crawls into bed and gathers me into his arms. "Sleep, Princess. I'll be here when you wake up." He kisses my hair and my eyes shut. I sigh and fall asleep before I can respond.

"You bitch. You'll pay for this." Theodore sneers and lifts a hand. I cower in front of him.

I look around and notice I'm back in my bedroom in California. I knew no jail could keep Theodore Abbot contained. My eyes stray to the closed door and he laughs.

"Go ahead. Try me. You won't get far."

Damn. He's right. There is not one person on the staff who will help me. They know if they do, ICE will sweep in and arrest each and every one of them.

And if I somehow manage to escape the house without the staff ratting me out, where would I go? The mansion sits on several acres of land outside the city. And I'm dressed in, I look down, a sheer nightgown. Great. I'm stuck.

"Now. Come here." He hooks his finger and gestures for me.

"No."

His eyes narrow as he walks to me. He grabs my hair and I scream.

"Princess. Wake up."

My eyes fly open and I search the room. I'm not back in the mansion. I'm in the apartment above McGraw's Pub. It was a dream. It wasn't real. Theodore isn't here.

"Shush, baby, you're safe." Ryker rocks me back and forth as he cradles me in his arms.

My breath hitches as my eyes fill.

"Let it go, Princess. Let it all go."

My tears tumble out and down my face. I sob and the stream of tears becomes a torrent. "He… he…"

"He can't get to you. Never again. You hear me. Never again." And with Ryker's strong arms around me, I believe him.

It takes a while, but with Ryker rubbing circles on my back, the stream of tears comes to a stop. I sniff and rub my eyes. I must look like hell. Great. I finally have Ryker right where my body wants him, and I look like doggy doo-doo.

But Phoebe 2.0 knows life is short. She's not wasting an opportunity when it lands in her lap. I tilt my head back and stretch my neck to touch my lips to his. As soon as our lips meet, I shiver. Nothing has ever felt better than his lips on mine. I deepen the kiss and force my tongue into his mouth. Ryker growls and rolls me so I'm laying on my back with him on top of me. *Yes.*

My hands explore his shoulders and back. I can feel his muscles pulled taut underneath my fingers, but I want to feel his skin. I grip the hem of his Henley and pull up until he's forced to break the kiss so I can remove it. My eyes widen when I see the layers upon layers of muscles on his chest. I lift a finger and poke his pec muscle. It's rock hard.

He smirks before brushing a hand down my cheek. "I think we should stop."

"Don't you want me?"

He responds by grabbing my hand and placing it on the front of his jeans. I feel a hard bulge and squeeze. He groans.

"Stop. I don't want to take advantage of you."

"Take advantage of me?" I giggle. "I'm practically throwing myself at you."

He brushes a strand of hair away from my forehead. "You just went through a trauma. You're not thinking clearly."

I'm not thinking clearly? I've never thought more clearly in my life. "I want you. I've wanted you since you kissed me in the foyer in front of everyone weeks ago." Earlier than that if I'm being totally honest.

"And I've been a complete dick since then."

I'm not going to disagree with him. Kidnapping me – even if it wasn't to take me back to my ex-husband like I thought at the time – puts him clearly in the dick category. "But I forgave you."

His eyes shut and all the tension in his body disappears. "Thank you," he says. When he opens his eyes, they're soft. Is that devotion I see?

"You sure?" Am I sure about what? I can't think with his body caging me in and him staring at me like I'm the best Christmas present he ever opened.

He growls and flexes his hips. I feel his hard cock press against me, and I wrap my legs around him to keep the delicious pressure right where I need it. My panties flood with excitement and my belly dips.

I bite my lip before gathering my courage and responding, "Show me I wasn't wrong to forgive you."

He kisses my nose before crawling slowly down my body with his eyes on mine the entire time. I squirm and he smirks. His hands move to unsnap my jeans before lowering the zipper. I bite my lip as anticipation flows through me causing my nerves to tingle and my stomach to heat.

He pulls my jeans off me and throws them on the floor. His fingers toy with the skin right above my panties before his head dips to lick and bite the area. I grab his head and force him to look up at me.

"No foreplay. I want you in me." My face heats as I say words I've never thought before let alone said.

He shakes his head. "Princess, I'm not a small guy."

"And I'm not a small woman."

"I don't want to hurt you."

"You won't." I bite my lip and consider begging. In all those romance books I love to read, begging always causes the big alpha man to give in. "Please."

He closes his eyes as his body shudders. When his eyes open again, they are full of need and desire. *Yes!* He grabs my panties and rips them down my body before standing and shoving his jeans down his legs. His cock jumps out, thick and proud, and I gasp. He wasn't kidding about his size.

I watch as he rolls a condom on before crawling back onto the bed with me. My legs widen to accommodate him, and he settles between them. "You're sure?"

Is he kidding? I'm dying to know what it feels like to have him inside me. "Please."

His head dips and his lips find mine. As his tongue plunders my mouth, his cock finds my entrance and slowly enters me. He dips in and then retreats. I arch my back and raise my hips, silently begging for more. He slowly enters me again, going a bit further before retreating once again.

I whimper. I want to feel all of him.

"Patience, Princess. I'll give you what you need, but I won't hurt you. Ever."

Oh my. Those words. They make me shiver and a rush of excitement gushes from me and eases his entry. He pushes in and groans as he bottoms out. He pauses for a moment, giving me time to adjust to his size, before starting to glide slowly in and out of me. It feels amazing. Like nothing I've ever felt before.

Sex has always been an obligation. It was never an activity to be enjoyed. Oh sure, I've given myself orgasms before, but I've never had a man-made orgasm. Judging by the warmth in my belly and the tingling down below, things are about to change.

He grabs my right leg and pulls it up and out. Oh my god! At this angle, he can penetrate deep inside of me. My head falls back, and I moan. "Ryker."

"I know you're close. I can feel you squeezing my cock." He grunts as his strokes speed up. "Get there, baby. Can't last much longer."

He reaches down and pinches my clit. "Yes," I hiss as my release hits me. Stars explode behind my eyes as my body spasms.

Ryker's movements become erratic. He plants himself deep and growls, "Phoebe." I feel his entire body shudder before he collapses on me.

Those erotic romance books I secretly love to read are not wrong. Sex is awesome.

Chapter 30

Polite society isn't all it's made out to be. In other words, polite society can suck it. ~ Phoebe's rules for becoming a better person

"You fuckers," Pops says before dumping a pile of magazines on the table. When the pile hits the table with a thump, I jump.

Ryker snarls. "You scared Phoebe."

Pops wrinkles his brow as he studies me. "You still having nightmares? I thought with the big guy here in your bed, those nightmares would be gone by now."

I cringe. Everyone knows Ryker is sleeping beside me in bed but sleeping arrangements are not a topic of discussion in polite society. I look around the table at the group of ex-Army buddies swilling beer and eating chicken wings. What was I thinking? This is not polite society. Thank goodness.

Ryker has pretty much refused to leave my side since Theodore kidnapped me. He's not my shadow. No, he's a magnet attached to my hip. He refuses to go back to his own work because he 'can't leave my side'. It doesn't matter that Theodore was refused bail. He's sticking to me.

He's also driving me bonkers. Pretty soon I'm going to be the crazy one of the group, not Suzie. Don't get me wrong. I love how protective he is. It's sexy as all get out. When he bosses me around in bed with his deep, growly voice, I melt. Seriously. Complete puddle of goo. But outside of the bedroom, he needs to let me get on with my life.

"Have you considered seeing a therapist?" Lenny asks and I groan. Here we go again.

"I've been trying to get her to see one," Ryker says.

The words 'do not quit' were invented on his behalf. The guy does not give up. Great in bed. No, absolutely freaking fantastic in bed. There is literally nothing better in the world than a man who is determined to make sure you come once (sometimes twice) before he does. But his no quit mentally should stay in the bedroom where it belongs.

"I do not need to see a therapist. It's bad enough Theodore claims I'm mentally unstable, I don't need the group of you to say it as well."

"Do I look crazy?" Sid asks.

Is this a trick question? "Um, no?"

"Would you think less of me if went to a therapist?"

I snort. "Like you would ever see a therapist." Well, there is one reason he'd go to a therapist. "Unless you were trying to pick her up."

He wrinkles his nose. "No, I don't swing both ways. Although, there's nothing wrong with anyone who does." He looks in Lenny's direction. Wait. What? Is Lenny bi? Before I get a chance to ask, despite his sexual orientation being absolutely none of my business, Sid continues. "Phoebe, darling, I saw a *male* therapist when I got out of the military."

"Dude was messed up," Lenny explains. "Lost the love of his life while he was dicking around."

"Which wife number was that?" I tease.

"Number one. Always number one."

Well, shit. No wonder he's been married five times. He's trying to replace the love of his life who is irreplaceable.

"Anyway, this is not about my marriages." Sid glares at Lenny. "What I'm trying to say is it's okay to seek help. No one will think less of you for it. In fact, it takes a strong person to admit they need help."

I slump against Ryker. "Fine. I'll see a therapist." I look up at him. "Are you happy now?"

"Ecstatic," he murmurs before he leans down, and his lips meet mine.

"No making out at the table!" Barney shouts.

I pull away. "Mr. Dirty Joke can't handle a bit of tongue?" My eyes widen when I realize what I said. I slam my hand over my mouth as my cheeks heat.

Ryker chuckles as he pulls me close. He winks before opening his mouth, but Barney shouts before he gets a chance to speak.

"Stop!" He holds up his hand. "Don't you dare say you like a bit of tongue."

Wally clamps a hand over Barney's shoulder. "You'll have to excuse him. Someone hasn't gotten any for a while. He's starting to get grumpy."

Hailey rushes to the table and grabs my hand. "You have got to see this." She yanks me out of the booth and pulls me to a table near the bar.

"What—"

"Shush." She tilts her head to the side and winks. She looks like she's having a seizure. When I merely gaze at her in confusion, she speaks without moving her lips, "Suzie. Bar."

I look over to the bar where Suzie is sitting next to a man. They seem to be having an animated discussion. As I watch, she giggles and reaches over to slap his arm. I blink. Maybe I do need to see a therapist because I'm seeing things. When my eyes focus once again, I realize I'm not seeing things. Suzie is indeed laughing and giggling with a man.

"Is she flirting?"

"Suzie's version of flirting at least."

My mouth drops open as they stand and walk off to the pool tables in the back corner of the pub. Suzie hip-checks the man, her hands flying as she continues to talk.

"Never thought I'd see the day Suzie managed to hip-check someone without falling over."

"I know, right?" Hailey says as she watches them. "She's talking, walking, and using her hands. It's almost like Suzie pre-Toby."

Now she has my attention. "Suzie pre-Toby? Surely, Suzie was always a klutz." You can't wake up one day and suddenly be the biggest klutz in the world.

"Nope. Don't get me wrong, she's always been a little klutzy. But the inability to walk without falling over? That's a post-Toby occurrence."

"How does getting your heart broken cause you to be klutzy?"

Hailey doesn't answer my question and instead confesses, "I've been worried about her. With me getting married and now you having a man, I thought she'd lose her mind. Maybe things aren't as bad as I thought."

She's worried about Suzie? Her worrying makes no sense. Suzie is the most happy-go-lucky person I've ever met. Why is Hailey worried? Before I have a chance to voice my confusion, Aiden and Ryker join us.

"You want to eat here or hit up the pizza place?" Aiden asks.

"Are you kidding? I'm not leaving until I see how Pops responds to the junk mail prank."

"What if Pops doesn't respond today?"

Hailey rolls her eyes. "Of course, he's responding today. Why do you think he saved up all the mail order bride catalogs and newsletters from the Ferret Association of Connecticut?"

"There's a Ferret Association of Connecticut? What do they talk about? How to tame your ferret?"

"It's actually a non-profit with an extensive library about domestic ferrets." When everyone stares at her, she shrugs. "What? Those magazines were laying around the living room. I was bored."

She rubs her hands together as Pops walks out of the kitchen. "Here we go."

"Who ordered the fried egg and fries?" When Wally raises his hand, Pops slams the plate in front of him before handing out plates of burgers to the other men.

"What's going on?" I whisper.

"Wait for it."

I watch as Wally cuts into the yolk with his fork. Instead of the yolk oozing goodness, it goes flying across the table. Wally glares at it before dipping his finger in the yolk. After he licks his finger, he lifts his head to glare at Pops who flips him off.

"Serves you right. I don't need to order a bride in the mail. From the Ukraine no less."

I'm confused. "What was on his plate?"

"Apple slices, yogurt, and a peach half."

"Oh, that's cruel," Aiden says and Ryker nods in agreement.

"Hey! Some of those women were fine," Sid yells across the room.

"What happened? Nurse Mary Ann kick you to the curb?" Pops asks.

"They really don't care about airing their private lives in front of strangers, do they?" I ask as my head ping pongs left and right to watch their verbal volleys back and forth across the crowded bar.

"Please." Hailey snorts. "Men gossip worse than women."

Aiden wraps an arm around her shoulder and pulls her close. "Yeah, sure. And you didn't just drag Phoebe over here to gossip about your friend Suzie."

"We weren't gossiping. We were observing. I'm a PI. Watching and observing is the name of my game." She looks up at him. "Besides, you can't tell me the uncles didn't already ask you to do a background check on him." She thumbs her finger toward the man Suzie is playing pool with.

Aiden's cheeks pink. Hailey nods. "Exactly what I thought."

Ryker puts his arm around my shoulders and pulls me close to kiss my forehead. "You doing okay? The uncles kind of ambushed you back there."

"Don't act like you aren't happy I agreed to see a therapist."

"Busted."

I giggle. "At least you're honest. Or honest now, I should say." I can't help myself from bringing up his earlier treachery. It plays on a loop on my mind.

The smile dies on his lips and he pulls me close. "I told you before, but I'll repeat myself until you believe me. I won't lie to you again, Princess. There may be things I can't tell you about my job, but I won't lie to you again. Ever. Promise."

I shouldn't believe him. But after living with a man who could win an Olympic Gold Medal for Best Liar In the Universe, I like to think I can detect lies better than most women. And Ryker? He looks sincere. Besides, who would put up with the craziness surrounding my life if they weren't serious about me? Not to mention put his career on hold while protecting me.

"Okay," I whisper.

"Thank you," he mutters before his lips crash on mine. I immediately open up and his tongue pushes his way into my mouth. I nip him and he growls.

Hailey wolf whistles and I realize we're in the middle of a bar. I pull away from Ryker and look around. Everyone's staring at us with big smiles on their faces. Is this what it feels like to be part of a family? They may drive me crazy, but you won't hear me complaining. Not today at least.

Chapter 31

Ladies don't day drink. Good thing I'm no longer a lady. ~ Phoebe's rules for becoming a better person

"You're going the wrong way," I tell Ryker the next morning when he turns left instead of right on East Kilbourn Avenue.

His response? He grunts. Someone needs to learn grunting is not an answer.

"Where are we going?"

My eyes widen and I rub my hands in excitement when I get an idea. "Are you taking me with you to catch a skip?"

Ryker glances over at me with a look of confusion written all over his face. "You'd like that?"

I bob my head. "Yeah. It would be interesting. I could probably learn a thing or twenty from you as well."

Here's the thing. I started out in the whole private investigator business because Hailey and Suzie were willing to take a chance on me without asking for all kinds of information I couldn't give them. And they paid cash. Always a bonus when you're living under an assumed name.

But now that I've gone out on my own for some insurance claim cases, I've discovered I like the work. Sure, it can be boring sitting in a car outside someone's house for hours on end, but that's why podcasts were invented. And there is absolutely nothing like the feeling of capturing the 'gotcha picture' as Suzie refers to the pictures of the cheaters getting caught red-handed.

"Okay. I'll take you out on one condition."

"Anything." I can't agree quick enough.

"You follow everything I say. I don't chase insurance scammers. I chase criminals who are running from the law. It's dangerous."

Dangerous? I don't like the sounds of that. "But you're careful, right? You don't take unnecessary chances?"

Ryker reaches over and grabs my hand. "Are you worried about me, Princess?"

I roll my eyes. "Of course, I am. You're my boyfriend."

"I'm not your boyfriend."

Oh, shit. Have I misunderstood everything? This is what happens when you're forced to marry a man your parents choose for you. You have no experience in romantic relationships. I try to tug my hand away, but Ryker holds tight.

"I'm a thirty-five-year-old man. I'm not a boy."

No need to remind me. My feminine bits still tingle from where he showed me how much he isn't a boy this morning. The man has stamina. I rub my legs together at the reminder.

I gather my courage together and ask, "What are you then? If you're not my boyfriend?"

"I'm your man." He winks at me before returning his attention to the road.

I exhale a breath I didn't realize I was holding. I didn't misunderstand everything after all. Look at me, having social skills and everything.

"Where are we going?" I ask again once my heart has calmed.

"It's a surprise."

"A surprise? Don't tell me the big bad bounty hunter can be romantic."

Ryker shakes his head, but there's a grin on his face. "Only with you, Princess."

Yeah, right. Insert eye roll here.

He squeezes my hand. "No, seriously. You are the only woman I've ever made an effort for. I've never chased after a woman. Not to sound like a jerk, but I've never needed to."

Now I do roll my eyes. It isn't lost on me how all the women pant after him wherever he goes.

"You're not getting this. You're the woman I want to make the effort for. I don't care about other women. Only you."

Oh my. His words make me feel special. Do I say he is special to me as well? I've never had a boyfriend … er man … before, I don't know how this works.

Before I have a chance to straighten out my head, he announces, "We're here."

I look around. *I Did It My Way Distillery.* "What are we doing here?"

"I arranged a private tour since I know how much you love your vodka. I thought it'd be a good chance for you to try some good old American vodka and not the Russian swill you currently drink."

"Yeah!" I cheer. I've never been inside a distillery before despite owning shares in one.

I freeze with my hand on the door handle. Those shares are in my name, not Theodore's. In fact, all of the shares are in my name. And since Theodore is now behind bars, I don't have to worry accessing my stock portfolio will alert him as to where I am. Holy cow. I'm the rich girl again.

Ryker opens the door and pulls me into his arms. "What is it? What's wrong?" He scans the parking lot. "Did you see suspicious activity?"

"Um." I bite my lip. Should I tell him? Will he still want me if I am the spoiled little rich girl he thought I was when we first met? "Can we discuss this later?"

He frowns but nods. "Come on. I don't like being outside exposed like this."

We walk to the entrance where someone is waiting to welcome us. "Hi. I'm Ronald. I'll be your guide today. You must be Mr. and Mrs. Rossi."

They shake hands as I giggle. I nudge Ryker but he doesn't correct Ronald's misconception about our marital status. I shrug. Oh well. I guess it doesn't matter what Ronald thinks.

For the next hour, we follow Ronald through the distillery as he explains how they make the various spirits. *I Did It My Way* makes vodka, rum, gin, and whiskey. I don't pay much attention as he explains how they distill rum, gin, and whiskey. I perk up when it's vodka's turn.

They take making vodka seriously. They use all organic ingredients from local farmers and focus on taste instead of efficiency. Ronald looks straight at me when he claims big Russian vodka producers focus on efficiency. I guess someone told Ronald about my love of Stolichnaya. Ryker could have let me know it bothered him I drink Russian vodka instead of ambushing me, although I'm having entirely too much fun to call this an ambush.

Ronald then goes on to explain how vodka is a neutral spirit, but they try to give the drink a subtle hint of the underlying ingredients. He's officially piqued my curiosity. I can't wait to give it a try.

We finish the tour and end up in the bar which is still empty as they don't open until noon on weekdays and it's barely past eleven.

"Are you ready to try our rum?" Ronald asks.

Is he kidding? Did he not see how interested I was in the vodka distilling? He winks and grabs a bottle of vodka from the freezer below the bar. Then, he grabs three frosty shot glasses and fills them with vodka.

"I've never tasted vodka before. I mean, I've drunk vodka, obviously. But is there a special way to taste it?"

Ronald chuckles. "First, hold it in your hands to warm it up slightly."

I grab the cold glass and shiver.

"Now, smell the vodka as you swirl it in your glass."

I swirl my glass and take a sniff. "It smells grainy."

Ronald smiles. "That's good. You don't want it to smell medicinal or like ethyl." He lifts his glass. "Now hold the glass up to the light and look at the clarity."

"It looks slightly bluish. I thought it should be clear." But obviously, I know nothing about my favorite drink.

"A tint of color, like blue or yellow, is good. Vodka should have an internal energy."

An internal energy? Is this where we get the sales pitch? I cut him off at the pass. "Are we going to actually taste the vodka?"

His smile widens. "Take a sip and let the vodka rest on your palate while exhaling through your nose. Then, swallow and take note of the aftertaste."

I do as he says. My eyes widen as the taste explodes on my tongue. I forget all about the resting on the palate business and swallow. "Yummy."

Ryker snickers. I frown when I see his glass is empty. He shrugs. "I know I like it. I don't need to taste it."

"I was going to suggest having a sip of water and then downing the rest of the shot to compare the two tastes, but I guess we can skip that step."

I giggle at Ronald's frowning face.

"Now, I'm going to teach you how to make some of the most popular vodka cocktails."

By the time we leave the distillery two hours later, I've learned how to make a vodka martini, cosmopolitan, and a Moscow mule. I've also drank more vodka in a single day than most people drink in a year. I may stumble as Ryker leads me across the parking lot to his truck.

"Thank you," I gush once he manages to get me into the passenger seat. "This was awesome. Even if you didn't have a good time."

Ryker wasn't into making cocktails. And he may have growled a time or two when Ronald put his hands on me for instruction purposes. Jealous Ryker is super hot.

"Anything for you, Princess."

I sigh and promptly pass out in his truck.

Chapter 32

Hangovers suck. That's it. That's my kern of
wisdom for the day. ~ Phoebe's rules for
becoming a better person

"Princess," Ryker whispers in my ear as he shakes my shoulder. I slap his hand away.

"No. Go away." My head is killing me. Whoever said you can't get a hangover from drinking vodka is a big fat liar.

He kisses the side of my head. "It's nearly lunchtime. Don't you need to get to work?"

Shit. I roll over and slowly sit up in bed. The room spins for a moment before Ryker's smirking face comes into focus. I point my finger at him.

"I blame you. You were the one who took me day drinking on a school day."

He chuckles before grabbing my hands and hauling me to my feet. His lips briefly touch mine before he pulls away. "Come on. Hailey called. She wants your help on a case."

I perk up. I love working on cases with Hailey – assuming she doesn't bring Lola with her. She may be cute as all get out, but the word horny was invented for that dog. I dress as quickly as my shaky legs will allow.

Once we're on the road to *You Cheat, We Eat,* I dial Hailey's number, but she doesn't pick up. I bite my lip and tap my foot. I hope she's not mad at me for coming in late.

Ryker pats my leg to still my nervous tapping. "Stop worrying. You're not an office worker and you don't get paid a salary. You don't have to be in the office at 9 a.m. every morning."

I know he's right, but I hate how I missed a call from Hailey. What if she needed back-up? No more day drinking.

I'm practically running and dragging Ryker with me when I open the door to the office.

"Surprise!" Suzie shouts and I freeze.

I look around but I don't see anything out of the ordinary. I wrinkle my brow. "Surprise what?"

Hailey rolls her eyes. "I told you not to overdo it."

"Go big or go home!" Suzie raises her fist in the air.

"What's going on?"

"Maybe you should go check out your office," Suzie sings and points to my office door. My closed door. I never close my door.

I take a deep breath to brace for whatever shenanigans she's up to now and walk to the door. Before I open it, I look around at their smiling faces. They're not punking me, are they? I know Hailey loves practical jokes. It's an inherited trait as her pops is always pulling pranks. I've learned to sniff my shampoo before using it. The man may be sweet as all get out, but he's a troublemaker. Beer does not belong in shampoo.

I open the door and frown. "Why is my office filled with filing cabinets?"

Suzie skips up behind me. "Because it's not your office anymore."

My heart stops. "Not my office. Are you firing me? I have my license now."

Hailey pushes Suzie out of the way. "Ignore her." She grabs my hand and guides me to the door of the filing room. "This," she points to the door, "is your new office."

She opens the door and I gasp. This room was filled with boxes and filing cabinets a mere two days ago. Now, there are two desks on opposite sides of the room with visitor chairs in front of them. I sniff. It smells like there's a fresh coat of paint as well.

"Are we sharing an office now?" I ask Hailey.

"Nope. You'll be sharing your office with someone else." She winks. Why is she winking? I'm not getting the joke.

"Did you hire a new investigator?" I'm a bit disappointed she didn't involve me in the hiring process. I know I haven't been at the PI firms long, but we're a team. Big decisions like hiring new personnel should be done as a group, right?

Ryker comes up behind me and twirls me around to face him. "She didn't hire me, but I'll be renting an office as well as some administrative services from the firm."

"What in the world are you talking about? You're a bounty hunter, not a PI."

He grabs my hands and pulls me into the office where he forces me into a chair. "I need a base of operations that isn't the back of my truck."

Don't get me started on the back of his truck. The man keeps all sorts of things in his backseat, including his files.

"And I'm not leaving Milwaukee anytime soon."

My heart hammers at his words. I've kept my mouth shut as I didn't want to interfere with his career, but I've been worried he would come out one day and say it's time for him to get back to work and take off. Dare I hope he's serious?

"You're staying?"

His smile stretches from ear to ear and his dimple comes out to play. "When is it going to get through your head? I'm not leaving you." He lifts his hand and tucks a piece of my hair behind my ear. He squeezes my neck and pulls my head forward until his forehead touches mine. "I love you, Princess. I'm not leaving."

Every nerve ending in my body ignites as butterflies awake in my stomach. "You love me?"

He smirks. "Yeah, babe. What do you think we're doing here?"

Like I have a clue. Relationships are not my forte as evidenced by my staying with Theodore for nearly a decade. "I…"

I have no idea what to say. It's a reflex for me to respond to *I love you* with *I love you too*, but do I love him? I think I do, but what do I know about love? In the past, love was used as a weapon against me. *If you love us, you'll marry Theodore.* And my all-time favorite – *If you love me, you won't embarrass me tonight.*

"Are you done making out yet?" Suzie walks into the room with her hand covering her eyes and promptly runs into a desk. She bounces off it like she's playing bumper cars.

"You can drop your hand. We're decent."

"Not by choice," Ryker grumbles.

My eyes widen. "Are you serious?" I whisper. "She listens at the door, you know."

"Don't care."

A dog rushes into the room, lifts up his leg, and a stream of pee hits the corner of one of the desks. "What the hell? Who's this? Where's Lola?"

Hailey runs into the room. She grimaces when she sees the puddle of pee. "Aiden couldn't bear the thought of having Lola sterilized. He decided she needed a boyfriend to 'tame' her."

"How's that working out?" I ask despite being able to see and smell how it's clearly *not* working out. "I'm not cleaning up after him."

"Leroy." She slaps her hands on her thighs. "Come here, boy." Leroy looks at her and barks before running to the corner where he commences playing with a dust ball.

"Aiden promised Leroy was housebroken. Aiden's sleeping in the doghouse tonight."

Hailey stomps to the corner and grabs her dog by the collar. She drags him out of the room. The dog thinks it's all a game. He yips and nips at her hand while trying to escape.

"Hey! Who's going to clean up the pee?" I shout after her. "Well." I raise my brows at Ryker. "What do you think of your new office now?"

"I'm good. My favorite person in the world is here."

"Ah." Suzie places a hand over her forehead and feigns a swoon. "Isn't he adorable?"

"Yeah, the big bad bounty hunter is adorable."

"Now, get out of here and celebrate him telling you he loves you for the first time." Suzie wiggles her brows.

"Told you she was listening at the door."

Ryker stands. "Actually, I've got shit to do. Barney's going to keep watch on you until I can get back."

I groan. "Barney?" Ugh. The entire afternoon is going to be wasted listening to him tell dirty jokes.

Ryker smirks as he leans forward to kiss my forehead. "Don't worry. He'll keep you safe."

I'm not worried about my safety. I'm worried about my sanity.

The alarm beeps as the front door opens. "Honey, I'm home. Who's ready for some spice in their life?" I can practically hear Barney wiggle his eyebrows. Ugh.

As soon as Ryker leaves, Hailey grabs my hand and pulls me into her office.

"Slow down. Where's the fire?"

She points a finger at Barney. "Stay."

He rolls his eyes but doesn't move from his spot as sentry in front of the door.

Suzie follows us into Hailey's office and closes the door behind her. "What are we doing?" she whisper-shouts.

"We're making sure our girl isn't freaking out since the man she loves told her he loves her."

My mouth opens and all my worries pour out. "I'm totally freaking out. It's Ryker. Have you seen the man? Why would he love a woman like me? I'm such a mess and trouble follows me wherever I go." I point to the door. "Case in point? There's a man guarding the door."

Suzie squeals and jumps up and down. "She didn't deny she loves him." She starts dancing around. "Phoebe and Ryker sitting in a tree. K-I-S-S-I-N-G."

I ignore the crazy lady and collapse in a chair. "I can't love him. I don't know what love is."

Hailey snorts. "Of course, you do." I open my mouth to explain – once again – how my parents never showered me with love like her pops does with her, but she stops me with a raised hand.

"Does he make you want to be a better person? When you thought he was hurt when that car barreled to a stop in front of him were you terrified for him? Does his pain hurt worse than yours? Do you want to spend the rest of your life with him?"

Her questions hit me like an arrow to the heart. Oh shit. Do I love him?

"And what about the sex?" Suzie asks. "You can't have bad sex for the rest of your life."

Hailey rolls her eyes. "Have you seen Ryker? If that man doesn't give good sex, then I have no faith in the male species."

I'm too busy freaking out about loving Ryker to explain how he doesn't give good sex. No, he gives great sex. The best I've ever had. Although – honestly – that's not saying much.

"Earth to Pheebs. Earth to Pheebs."

"I love him," I whisper. "When did this happen?"

"I'm guessing when he admitted he kidnapped you to protect you from your ex. Or maybe when he saved you from Theodore. And then there was the time he stood up to the uncles on your behalf." Suzie shrugs. "Honestly, there's a lot of good stuff to pick from."

Oh no. I plant my face in my hands. "He told me he loves me, and I didn't say it back. I'm a total bitch."

"No biggie. You can tell him anytime." Hailey sits in the chair next to me. "In fact, we should plan a romantic evening for you to tell him."

Suzie is all for it, meaning we get absolutely no work done for the rest of the day as we're too busy concocting and dismissing 'romantic' plans. As the hours slide by, my nerves get worse and worse until I'm practically vibrating with anxiety. I've never told a man I love him and meant it. I'm terrified I'm going to mess it all up.

Chapter 33

John Lennon was right. Life is what happens when you're busy making plans. ~ Phoebe's rules for becoming a better person

RYKER PULLS ON MY hand to stop me. "I don't think you should go."

We've been over this a thousand times already. "I have to go. I need to see this through."

Theodore struck a deal with the district attorney. I cannot believe he's going to plead guilty. Of course, he's not pleading guilty to kidnapping – a crime he definitely committed. Instead, he agreed to plead guilty to assault and battery and false imprisonment in exchange for a lesser sentence.

I know the criminal justice is overworked and trials cost tons of money, but this plea bargain doesn't seem fair to me. Theodore will spend a mere five years in prison, less with good behavior. He kidnapped me, punched me in the jaw, and drugged me. If Ryker hadn't saved me, he would have forced me into a plane and fled across state lines.

And then there's the arson. He set fire to Sid's place. He might not have lit the match, but he certainly ordered the arson to be committed. Those charges were dropped to my frustration. My testimony and recording were deemed inadmissible for reasons I cannot begin to fathom. Sid doesn't seem to care. His little romance with Nurse Mary Ann is back on and he's happy as a clam.

Today is Theodore's plea hearing and I insisted on attending. Ryker is less than happy about the situation. I don't care. I'm done altering my behavior to please other people. Besides, I need to see with my own two eyes as Theodore is taken to prison. Only then will I believe this is over and I can move on with my life.

"I don't like this," Ryker grumbles as we enter the courthouse.

Yeah, yeah, tell it to someone who cares. I ignore him. He's been bitching and moaning about this hearing for days now. He hates being unable to protect me since he can't carry his gun into the courthouse. If I've told him once, I've told him two gazillion times – nothing is going to happen to me in a courthouse full of security guards and police.

Once we make it through the metal detector, another thing my big bad bounty hunter gripes about the entire time, we walk up the stairs to the courtroom. Ryker tries to pull me into a seat in the back. No way. Nuh-uh. This girl is done cowering from Theodore. I march to the front row and sit directly behind the prosecutor.

We sit through two plea hearings before the bailiff announces the next case on the docket is State vs. Abbot. I glare as Theodore saunters into the room with a guard at his back.

I'm disappointed he's not in prison orange but apparently, it's normal to allow defendants to change for court hearings.

When he looks at me and smirks, I nearly lose it. Ryker's hand squeezing my thigh is the one thing stopping me from standing and screaming at the man. I now understand why you can't bring weapons into a courthouse. I can barely resist the temptation to steal the guard's gun, so I can bash Theodore over the head with it.

Fifteen minutes later, we're standing outside the courthouse. I'm in a daze. The entire process took less time than a manicure. And I didn't get the chance to see Theodore hauled away in handcuffs. Since the Christmas holidays are nearly upon us, he was remanded on bail until the new year when he'll start his sentence. I call bullshit.

Ryker guides me to his truck and lifts me into the passenger seat. He cradles my face. "Are you okay, Princess?"

I don't know. Honestly, I have no clue. I'm not sure if I'm let down, relieved, angry, or what. Obviously, I'm confused.

He squeezes my neck. "Baby, talk to me. I knew coming here was a bad idea."

Those are exactly the words I need to hear to pull me out of my funk. "Don't you dare. It was my right and choice to come here today. I just need time to process everything is all."

He studies my face for a minute before nodding and dropping his hand. "I was going to wait, but I have a surprise for you."

I perk up. "A surprise? What is it?" I look around the truck, but I don't spot anything unusual.

Ryker chuckles before shutting the door and rounding the truck. "You'll see," he says as he starts the engine. We leave downtown and drive north to the Upper East Side.

"Where are we going?" I ask as I look around the residential street we're driving on.

Ryker doesn't respond as he parks in front of a gray Victorian house with white trim. It has a wraparound porch upon which a pair of red Adirondack chairs sit. It's an adorable house, but I still haven't the first clue what we're doing here.

"What's this?"

"Come on. Let me show you the place." He jumps out of the truck before I can ask him whose place this is and what it has to do with me.

I follow him up the sidewalk to the porch. He pulls a key out of his pocket and opens the front door before ushering me inside. We walk into a large foyer with wooden floors and a sweeping staircase.

Ryker grabs my hand and tugs me through French doors into the living area. On one side is a fireplace with recessed bookshelves on each side. Kitty-corner to the fireplace is a bay window with a window seat spanning the width of the room. The seat looks like the perfect place to cuddle up with a book in the winter.

I drop Ryker's hand as I walk through another set of French doors into the dining room, beyond which is the kitchen. I don't know how to cook, but if I did, this is the kitchen I'd want to cook in. The Shaker cabinets are painted white to offset the gray granite countertops. The wood floors gleam and the stainless-steel appliances shine.

I continue through the house to the second floor where I discover the master bedroom. My bedroom in California might have been bigger but this room is cozy and warm compared to *that* place. There's another fireplace in here as well as sliding doors onto a balcony overlooking the backyard. The backyard is fenced in and at the end of the yard is a separate garage.

I explore the rest of the upstairs and discover there are four bedrooms in total. But I still don't know what I'm doing here. I walk back downstairs and discover Ryker lounging on the sofa.

"What do you think?"

"What do I think? I think you should get off the furniture." I don't know what we're doing here but sitting on someone else's furniture is a no-no unless you're invited to sit.

He ignores me to ask a question of his own. "Do you like the place?"

"It's gorgeous and charming and homey. Of course, I like it." My eyes widen as Ryker lifts his feet and places them on the coffee table.

I rush to him and push his feet off the table. Or at least I try to. The man refuses to budge. "Are you out of your mind? You're being incredibly rude."

"Who am I being rude to?"

"Duh. To whoever owns this house."

He smirks. "Guess I'm not being rude then."

I'm an idiot. I should have figured this out sooner. In my defense, this isn't the type of house I would expect the big guy to buy. A log cabin in the middle of nowhere seems more like his style.

"This is your place?" I ask although I'm pretty sure I know the answer.

He nods. "What do you think of the décor and furniture?"

I look around the room at the eggshell walls and gray trim. It's classic and not what I would have expected of Ryker, but it fits the old Victorian house. "I like it, but it's more important you like it. You're the one who will live here after all."

He chuckles. "Babe. I bought this house for us."

"You did what now?"

He drops his feet and grabs my hand to pull me close. "I know I should have involved you in the decision, but I didn't want to pressure you or make you feel uncomfortable. I know you don't have much money right now."

I look away. Shit. I need to tell him about my stock portfolio. "Actually …" I trail off. I don't know how to tell him I own a ton of stock.

He grasps my chin and forces me to look at him. "What is it, Princess? Do you not like the house after all? Am I moving too fast?"

"You probably are moving too fast, but you won't hear me complaining."

He smiles and I temporarily forget I need to share news with him. He rarely smiles, so when I manage to make him smile, I feel like I can conquer the world.

"What is it then, Princess?"

"I have a stock portfolio," I blurt. "It's worth a lot of money." I cringe as I wait for his reaction.

His brow wrinkles. "But you've been living in a shithole and selling your clothes for money."

"I was afraid to touch it before. I was worried if I cashed in some of my stock, Theodore would find me. But there's no need to worry about him finding me anymore."

"Okay." He nods. "Now, tell me more about these stocks."

"What do you want to know?"

He clenches his jaw and I can hear his teeth grinding. "I want to know if you're going to go back to your cushy life since you have money. I want to know how you could ever live in this house since—"

I cut him off when my lips meet his. I pour everything I'm feeling but have been too chicken to say into the kiss. He doesn't let me be in charge for long. He pulls me onto his lap and wraps his hand around my neck to tilt my head to his liking.

My body heats and my breasts swell. I can feel his cock growing and thickening underneath me. I grind myself on him and sparks ignite in my belly. Suddenly, he yanks my head away.

"Before we christen this couch, I need to know you're staying."

"Of course, I'm staying. I love you. I'm not going anywhere."

His eyes turn soft. "You love me?"

Oh shit. "I had this whole romantic evening planned out to tell you."

"Princess, I don't need romance. I only need you."

"And you have me."

His eyes sparkle with happiness before he announces, "We'll save the stocks for our children."

"Children?"

"Yeah. Why do you think this house has four bedrooms?"

My eyes widen. "You want children?"

"I never thought about children before you. But a kid with your eyes and smile? I want a whole bunch of those."

I worry my lip between my teeth. "I'm not sure about children."

Don't get me wrong. I've always wanted children, but after your ex-husband kidnaps you with the intent of forcing you to have his children, the idea kind of loses its appeal.

"Hey." Ryker smooths a finger over a wrinkle on my forehead. "No pressure. If you don't want children, we won't have them. I can change one of the rooms into a gym. And I should probably get a man cave to hide in when I piss you off."

"Plan on pissing me off often?"

He shrugs. "I'm a man, you're a woman. I'm sure I'll stick my foot in my mouth on a regular basis."

I grin. I'm sure he will.

"You good?" I nod. "You love me?"

I blush but maintain eye contact. "Yes."

"Good." His lips descend and meet mine. I sigh and he thrusts his tongue into my mouth. My tongue duals with his as I grind down on his hard cock. He wrenches his mouth from mine and stands with me in his arms. "Time to christen the bedroom."

Yeah!

Chapter 34

Don't let yourself be steamrolled. Unless you want to be steamrolled. ~ Phoebe's rules for becoming a better person

I ROLL OVER AND frown when I encounter an empty bed. Darn it. I forgot Ryker moved into his new house. You can't buy a house and then not live there. I'm an idiot for thinking he'd still sleep beside me, although he did stay with me last night until I fell asleep.

I force myself to my feet and paste a smile on my face. Today is Saturday, which means Pops will be roaming around the apartment and I have no work to escape to. I can't let him see how bummed I am Ryker isn't staying with me any longer. His idea for cheering me up involves copious amounts of food. I'm not going to fit into my clothes much longer considering all the 'loving' he's thrown at me since I moved in a couple of weeks ago.

I shuffle into the kitchen and freeze when I see Pops and Ryker glaring at each other.

"What's going on?"

Pops crosses his arms over his chest and leans back against the kitchen counter. "Go ahead. Tell her. Tell her what you planned without consulting her."

Ryker's nose flares. "It's a surprise. How can I consult her when I'm trying to surprise her?"

The apartment door bangs open and Lenny, Barney, Sid, and Wally stroll in. I groan. It's entirely too early for six alpha males.

"Hey, Phoebe, what do you call—"

I hold up my hand to stop Barney from continuing with his corny joke. "It's too early for you."

"That's what she said!" Sid says and holds up his hand for a high-five.

I shake my head. "I haven't had coffee yet." And I'm in my pajamas. At least I remembered to put on a robe.

Ryker hands me a cup of coffee and kisses my forehead. "Good morning, Princess."

I melt into him and he wraps his arm around my waist and pulls me close. I get a warm feeling in my belly like this is where I belong. Among a bunch of potty-mouthed men who take being protective to the nth degree. The family I was born into was a mistake of fate. Those are not my people. I look around at the smiling faces of the uncles. These are my peeps.

Wally rubs his hands together. "You ready to move?"

Ready to move? Maybe I was wrong. Maybe this isn't where I belong.

Ryker growls. "I haven't told her yet."

Pops growls right back to him. "And I told you it's too soon."

I raise my hand like I'm in a classroom. "Can someone tell me what's going on?"

Ryker spins me around. His eyes go warm as he looks down at me. He places a hand on my cheek. "You're moving into our home today."

"Our home? Today?" My words make no sense because nothing makes any sense.

"Yeah. The house I showed you yesterday. Where you told me you loved me."

"Pay up, fuckers," Sid announces. "I told you she loved him."

Lenny snorts. "Dude. Everyone with eyes can see they love each other. Why do you think we tolerate him?"

"Can the crazy train pull into the station for a second, so I can hop on?" Wait a second. I'm not making sense. I don't want to get *on* the crazy train.

Ryker grabs my hand and pulls me down the hallway into my bedroom. He shuts the door, locks it for good measure, and then pushes me onto the bed. He kneels in front of me before taking my hands again.

"I know this is fast. I know this is crazy. But I don't want to sleep at night without you. I want to wake up in the morning to your beautiful face. I want to be waiting each evening for you to come home and tell me about whatever crazy shenanigans you and Hailey and Suzie got up to. I want to share my life with you."

Those wings battering around my stomach aren't butterflies. No, a mother freaking albatross has taken over my stomach. Dare I believe his words?

He releases my hand and places his palms against my cheeks and leans in close. "I love you, Phoebe. This is what love is. Wanting to share every moment with a person."

I close my eyes and lean my forehead against his. "I'm scared."

Ryker doesn't belittle me. No, he moves right on to finding a solution. "Talk it out. Why are you scared?"

"I've never been this happy before. What if it's a mirage?"

"Princess, open your eyes." I force my eyes open to see Ryker smiling at me with soft eyes. He grabs my hands and places them over his heart. Ba-bump. Ba-bump. "You feel that?" I nod. "This heart beats for you. I'm not going to say every single moment of our lives will be happy. It would be a lie. But I promise you right here, right now I will do my damndest to make you happy every single day of your life."

My eyes burn and I can feel tears swell.

Ryker raises an eyebrow in question. "What do you say? Will you move in with me?"

I bite my lip and bob my head. He leans in and melts his lips to mine, but he withdraws way too early for my liking.

"Let's get you packed up and moved."

"Someone better supervise the uncles before they start pulling pranks. I don't want to wake up to a ghost flying into the bedroom or whatever else they can think of."

Ryker slaps my bottom as I stand. "There's my girl."

We spend the rest of the morning packing up my things and moving me into the adorable Victorian house. There isn't much to pack at Pops' place, except a ton of clothes. Thanks to my discovery of discount department stores, I've been able to replenish my wardrobe after selling most of my clothes for money. While Ryker and I deal with my clothes and other incidentals, the uncles load up my furniture from the boarding house and bring it to the new place.

"Why are you keeping that crap?" I ask Ryker as he directs the uncles to carry my sofa to one of the empty spare bedrooms. "It's cheap. We don't need to keep it."

Ryker prowls to me. "Princess, I want you to understand you have options. If you decide to leave—"

"I—"

He lays a finger over my lips. "Hear me out. I know when you left Theodore you couldn't take your things with you. I want you to have your things just in case."

I shake my head and wrap my arms around him. I tilt my head up and look at him. "I'm not leaving you. And I definitely don't need some ugly ass furniture as a reminder of how I struggled for the past year."

I don't bother reminding him I have a stock portfolio worth more money than I will ever need should I completely lose my mind and decide to run again.

Ryker studies my eyes for a moment before nodding. He raises his head to order the uncles to get rid of the furniture. They're already coming back down the stairs with my sofa.

"We heard you. We'll load her furniture up and take it to Goodwill," Wally says as he and Lenny carry the sofa out of the house.

"Now, don't you have a walk-in closet to take over?" Ryker asks once they've left.

"I sure do." I peck him on the lips before bouncing up the stairs to the master bedroom. The bedroom is all dark grays and blues now, but I'll add a feminine touch as soon as I get a chance to cash some of my stocks.

The walk-in closet is bigger than I expected considering the size of the house. It's practically the size of the smallest spare bedroom. And it's nearly empty. Ryker has filled less than a third of the area with his clothes. Does the man own any clothing other than jeans and black and gray shirts?

I spend the next hour emptying my suitcases and placing my clothes in the closet. When I finish, there's still some space remaining. I giggle. The old Phoebe would be appalled she didn't fill her closet to the brink. The old Phoebe was kind of materialistic. Phoebe 2.0 doesn't care about clothes. I lie. Of course, I still care about clothes. I am a girl after all.

Ryker knocks on the closet before sauntering in. He looks around with a grin on his face. "Looks good, Princess."

I stand and brush my hands on my jeans. "I'm all done."

He reaches forward for my hand. "I have a surprise for you."

I clap. "Yeah. What is it?"

He wiggles his hand. "Join me and I'll show you."

I clasp his hand and he leads me to the stairs. I shout when I see the massive Christmas tree now adorning the entranceway. I rush down the stairs for a closer look.

"Oh, my goodness. When did you do this? How long was I in the closet?"

Ryker chuckles as he joins me. "We only put up the tree. It still needs ornaments and lights and all the other Christmas stuff."

I can feel the telltale sign of tears welling in my eyes. "You left the decorating for me?"

He shrugs and a light pink colors his cheeks as his eyes rove around the room avoiding my gaze. "I thought we could decorate it together. Start our own Christmas tradition."

The tears now flow down my cheeks as I fly at him. "Thank you. I've never decorated a tree before."

I peck kisses on his cheeks until he growls and takes over. His lips crash to me and I immediately open up. His tongue invades and I sigh as his distinct spicy flavor hits me. I could kiss him forever, but he pulls away. I mewl in protest.

He smiles down at me. "We need to go to the store and buy decorations if you want to trim the tree today."

The disappointment at having his body taken away from me disappears at the idea of decorating the tree. I squeal and rush to the living room to grab my coat I threw over the couch. I freeze when I notice the living room has been completely transformed.

Instead of looking like a showroom, it now looks cozy. A plush light-pink afghan is draped over the sofa, which is now adorned with pink and cream colored pillows. The coffee table now sports a Christmas decoration with reindeers, red and white candles, pinecones, and red and gold ornaments.

"Who did this?"

"Suzie and Hailey came by while you were upstairs."

I can't believe Suzie was here and I didn't notice. And she didn't burn the place down.

"What do you think of the bookshelves?"

The bookshelves? I hadn't noticed them yet. I look over to see the bookshelves on each side of the fireplace are now filled with books and DVDs. I walk closer to read the titles. *Harry Potter, Lord of the Rings.* All of my favorites.

"How did you know?" I ask as I draw my finger across the brand new books.

Ryker comes up behind me and pulls me into his arms. "Because I listen to you, Princess. I know you like to read and watch movies to escape. And while I hope you won't feel the need to escape from your new life, I thought they would bring you comfort."

"You thought of everything!" I shout and burst into tears.

"I love you, Princess."

Chapter 35

If the answer is no, ask again and again until it's yes. ~ Phoebe's rules for becoming a better person

I WAKE TO THE feel of someone sliding my pajama bottoms and underwear off of me. Merry Christmas to me! Apparently, Christmas morning is going to be as awesome as Christmas Eve.

Ryker and I spent Christmas Eve at home. We were tucked up all warm with the fireplace blazing while snow pelted down outside. We watched Christmas movies with only the lights from the Christmas tree illuminating the living room. Best Christmas Ever.

I still find it hard to believe this is my life. A little more than a month ago, it was Thanksgiving and I was unsure about where Ryker and I were heading. Then, he kidnapped me and broke my heart. And now, we're living together and he's showing me how wonderful life can be. The past month has been the definition of a whirlwind.

"Good morning," Ryker says in a voice gruff from sleep and I shiver.

"Morning." My voice comes out sounding breathy but, in my defense, he's licking and biting his way up my legs. His beard scrapes against my skin and goosebumps explode.

I spread my legs to give him better access. I'm all about being accommodating.

"Merry Christmas, Princess," he says before licking circles around my clit. I moan and grab his head to make sure he doesn't move away. He chuckles and the sound reverberates against my sensitive skin causing wetness to seep from me. His tongue moves to catch the excitement he caused.

"I love the taste of you. Sweet and spicy. Just like my girl."

His words cause a blush to spread across my body. He lifts his head and smirks. I roll my eyes at the proud look on his face. I push on his head to force him to get back to what he was doing. He smirks but dips his head.

My hands dig into his hair as he nibbles along the edges of my clit. I growl. "Stop teasing me."

He ignores me and continues to circle the area where I need him most. I lift my hips to force his tongue where I want it. He grabs my hips to still me. I squirm as tingles and warmth spread throughout my body. For some reason, him immobilizing me does it for me.

I release his hair and lift my hands to toy with my breasts. I pluck at my nipples and Ryker growls. I bite my lip to hide my grin. He always loses control when I play with myself. And I may use this tidbit of knowledge to get him to do what I want more often.

His tongue stops teasing me and plunges into me. My back arches and lifts off the bed as I moan. His tongue retreats, but before I can mewl in complaint, his fingers are there, and his tongue is suckling on my clit.

"Ryker," I groan as my body pulls taut and I explode.

As soon as my tremors subside, Ryker lifts his head. His eyes are sparkling with need. Works for me. I motion to him and he crawls up my body. My nerve endings sated mere seconds before, re-awaken.

He brushes the damp hair from my forehead. "I love you, Princess."

Ryker doesn't hesitate to tell me how he feels about me. It's a welcome change from the people in my previous life who only uttered the word 'love' when they wanted something from me.

"Love you, too, big guy."

His head dips and his lips meet mine in a slow, sweet kiss. When he lifts his head, his eyes pierce mine as he slowly enters me.

"Never had better," he declares when he's balls deep in me.

"Me either."

I pant and lift my legs to wrap them around his back. I squeeze and lift my hips in an effort to get him to hurry the heck up.

Ryker nips my lip in punishment. "Going to make sweet, slow love to you this morning."

Well, when you put it that way, who am I to complain? I'm smiling as his lips meet mine. He doesn't plunder. No, he worships my mouth as his hand skims over my breasts and stomach as if he's memorizing every inch of me. I feel treasured.

My hands move to do some exploring of their own. I trace his back muscles with my fingertips. He trembles under my touch. There is absolutely nothing like the feeling of making this big guy tremble. It makes me feel powerful. Not powerful in the way Theodore felt when he berated me, but powerful as in confident in our love and the effect I have on him.

Ryker tears his mouth away from mine. "I'm nearly there." He grunts as his strokes become erratic.

I open my eyes and watch as pleasure takes over his face until my own pleasure hits. My head falls back as my back arches and I moan.

Ryker collapses on me before rolling off and pulling me on top of him. I look up at him and declare, "Best Christmas ever."

He grins as he rubs a hand up and down my back. "Tell me what Christmas was like when you were growing up in California."

I growl and look away. Ryker has been pushing me to talk about my previous life since I moved in with him.

"Why do you continue to push me?"

"Why did you quit counseling after one session?"

"I promised I'd give counseling a go. I never promised to keep at it if it didn't work."

And the counselor totally creeped me out. I wasn't telling Ryker about Mr. Creepy Counselor, though. Who knows what Mr. Overprotective on Steroids would do if he found out the man creeped me out? I made up some lame excuse about counseling not working instead.

"I know the counselor creeped you out."

Wait. What? "Are you reading my mind?"

"Babe."

Ugh! I hate when he answers with babe. If it's the last thing I do on this earth, I will rid him of the habit.

He rolls so he's lying on top of me. "If you're not going to talk to a counselor, then you need to talk to someone. I want to be that someone."

I stare at him a moment. He's wearing the 'not giving up' look. I know fighting him will be futile.

"Fine. Holidays in my previous life were beyond stressful. Everything had to be perfect. Everyone had to look perfect. It was exhausting. Is that what you want to hear?"

He nuzzles my neck. "Staying home yesterday didn't bother you?"

I tug on his hair until he looks at me. "Are you not hearing me? I don't want stress. I want to spend time with you. Yesterday was perfect. I loved it."

His smile lights up his face. "Exactly what I wanted to hear." He reaches over and opens the drawer of his bedside table. He picks something out before slamming the drawer closed and returning his attention to me.

"Phoebe, will you make this holiday perfect for me by agreeing to become my wife?"

My mouth drops open and I do the perfect imitation of a gaping fish. My heart speeds up and my chest squeezes. Surely,

I didn't hear him correctly. "But we hardly know each other." And my previous marriage wasn't exactly a happy time. Plus, I'm not exactly divorced yet.

He shrugs. "I know I love you. What else do I need to know?"

Um, I'm sure I can think of something if he gives me a minute. But my brain isn't working yet, and my heart is still beating out of control. "I'm surprised you're asking. You pretty much demanded I move in with you."

Ryker chuckles as he slides the ring onto my finger. "If you didn't say yes, I was planning on using sex as a weapon."

My heart races. "I didn't say yes."

"Too late. The ring's on your finger now."

I roll my eyes. "You weren't asking, were you? You were demanding I marry you."

He ignores my snipe to ask, "Aren't you going to look at your ring?"

"I…" I'm at a loss for words. This is crazy. I'm still trying to wrap my head around the idea of marriage and he's pushing me to look at my ring.

My first marriage was dysfunctional with a capital D. After that disaster, I'm not exactly raring to give marriage another go.

Ryker taps my cheek with his finger until I give him my attention. "Princess, I am not Theodore. I am not going to take away your choices and keep you locked up in a gilded cage. I'm going to spend every single day of my life proving to you that you made the right choice when you took a chance on me. I love you."

I stare into his mossy green eyes. They're filled with sincerity and hope. Dare I take a chance on this man? The man who – once he got his head out of his ass – has made me his number one priority every second of every day? I bite my lip and nod.

His dimple makes an appearance before his mouth dips to meet mine in a sweet, innocent kiss. He pulls back and tilts his head toward my hand. "Now are you going to look at your ring?"

I lift my hand to see a shiny princess diamond and giggle. Of course, he got me a princess cut diamond. It's set in a dainty white gold band. "It's gorgeous. Thank you."

To my surprise, he rolls off of me and jumps out of bed. "Where are you going?"

"It's Christmas day. We're having lunch with the family."

My heart squeezes at his use of the word family. My 'real' family doesn't exist to me anymore. They haven't bothered to contact me since Theodore kidnapped me. I won't hold my breath waiting for an apology from them for forcing me to marry Theodore. I know better. They don't care about my welfare one little bit. But would it have been too much to call and check in on how I'm doing now they know where I am? Apparently, it would.

They didn't contact me after my lawyer approached them regarding moving my stock portfolio to a local broker either. I expected rage and anger. I got silence. Oh well, I have a new family now.

A family Ryker is a part of as well. It warms my heart to see the man who grew up in foster care being accepted by the uncles.

"You just want to brag about getting engaged!" I shout at Ryker's retreating figure.

"Babe. They already know."

"What?" I jump out of bed and rush to him, ready to start a fight.

"I had to ask Pops and the uncles for your hand in marriage, didn't I?"

The fight leaves me, and my eyes well up. Asking the men, I consider my family, even if they aren't my blood, for permission to marry me is probably the sweetest thing he's ever done. I sniff to stop the tears from forming.

"What did they say?"

"My ring's on your finger, isn't it?"

I look down at my hand. Yeah, it is.

Ryker nabs my hand. "Come on. I want a shower before we leave."

A shower with my fiancé sounds like the perfect continuation of this perfect Christmas day.

Chapter 36

Everyone needs a little bit of crazy on Christmas.
~ Phoebe's rules for becoming a better person

"Hold up." Ryker pushes past me to open the door to Mc-Graw's Pub for me since my hands are full with a dish of brownies I made.

My cooking and baking skills have improved somewhat since I moved in with Ryker. But don't ask me about the incident with the chicken and the fire alarm. How was I supposed to know you shouldn't use too much oil in a pan? The instructions said heat oil in the pan, not how much oil to use.

Baking cakes and pies is still beyond my skill set, but I can bake a mean tray of brownies. Adding chocolate chips and a bit of peanut butter can make nearly anything taste yummy.

Ryker fumbles with the packages in his hands to open the door. "You might have gone a little overboard with the presents, Princess."

I glare and stomp my foot. "Ryker Rossi, you are not going to shame me about buying Christmas presents. This is the first Christmas I have people I care about to buy presents for." I stand on my tiptoes and get in his face. "First Christmas ever."

The corners of his lips tip up in a barely there smile. "Okay, Princess. No more complaints."

"Darn straight. There will be no more complaints."

Confession. He's not wrong. I totally went overboard with gift buying. But Ryker bought me a house and put a ring on it. I was compelled to show my appreciation. The result of which was a Christmas tree bursting with gifts this morning. I bought Ryker an iPad, a car office organizer, some non-black clothes… Yeah, I totally went overboard.

I wasn't sure if I should buy gifts for the rest of the family, but then I decided I didn't care if they didn't return the favor. Giving presents shouldn't be about what you receive in return. I may have gone hog wild at the mall. In my defense, seeing all those zeroes in my bank account after a year of living on ramen noodles would make any mall-loving girl go a bit looney.

Ryker kisses my forehead before taking a step back and opening the door. I take one step inside and cheers of *congratulations* erupt. I blush. "Did you tell them you were proposing this morning?"

"Yep." Ryker puffs his chest out. I'm surprised he doesn't start beating it.

Hailey and Suzie rush me. I set the brownies on the nearest table before they get dropped in the upcoming attack. Hailey grabs my hands and pulls me to the booth furthest from the men.

"How did he propose?" she asks as she shoves me into a seat.

Suzie plops down across from me. "Was it romantic?"

I raise my eyebrow. "You don't like romance, remember?"

"I like romance well enough as long as it doesn't involve me."

"Come on, spill," Hailey urges. "We don't have much time before Ryker comes to claim you."

I look over and sure enough, Ryker is staring at us. I shake my head and mouth *I'm fine.* I don't think he cares.

"He sort of demanded I marry him."

"Were you naked?"

My eyes widen. "Why would you ask that?"

Suzie giggles and points at my face. "The blush says you totally were naked."

"Whatever. Do you want to see my ring?"

I raise my hand and wiggle it in front of their faces.

"Holy batman. He's not fooling around," Suzie says as she grabs my hand.

Hailey snorts. "What did you expect? He moved her into his house without asking after knowing her for like a minute. The man knows what he wants."

The door opens and Suzie looks up. She scowls at whoever entered. I look over. The man she was flirting with a while ago is standing in the doorway looking uncomfortable.

"What is he doing here?" She grits her teeth as she glares in his direction.

"Are you fighting with your boyfriend?" I tease.

She switches her glare to me. "He isn't my boyfriend."

"He's a boy who's your friend. I.e. boyfriend."

She stands and marches to him. I follow because I'm nosy. Besides, after Suzie bugged me about my past and stuck her nose where it didn't belong, she deserves my nosy behavior. Hailey is right on my heels.

"What are you doing here, Grayson?"

"His name is Grayson? Sexy," I whisper to Hailey who giggles and nods in agreement.

Ryker tags me around the neck. "You better not be calling another man sexy."

I slap him on the stomach. "Shush. I want to hear."

Pops walks out of the kitchen to greet Grayson. "Good to see you, son." They shake hands and Pops slaps him on the back. "Merry Christmas."

Suzie turns on Pops. "What's he doing here?"

"What's wrong? I thought you were friends."

"Friends, yes." She crosses her arms over her chest. "But Christmas is for family."

Pops shakes his head and walks off, apparently unwilling to deal with the crazy lady on Christmas day. I don't blame him.

The door opens behind Grayson and Aiden walks in with Leroy and Lola. Leroy yips when he sees Hailey and breaks free. He doesn't make it to her before he slides to a halt to sniff a table. His leg lifts up and he commences peeing.

"I literally just took him out," Aiden claims as he watches Leroy run off to the kitchen.

"Get a dog they said. It'll be fun they said. It'll pee everywhere, they didn't say," Hailey mumbles as she trails after her dog.

Aiden unleashes Lola and she makes a beeline for me. "Stop," Ryker orders and she skids to a halt. "No, Phoebe is mine. Find your own girl."

"Don't let Aiden hear you say that. He'll go off and buy a girl dog for Lola to play with, and Hailey will kill you in her sleep."

He tugs me close. "I'm not worried. You'll save me."

"If I have to clean up doggy pee one more time, I may let her have you." Despite claiming I wouldn't be cleaning up after Leroy at the office, there's not a lot I can do about it when he pees on one of your desks. And the big guy pulls a disappearing act every single time it happens. Every dang time.

"Get over here, Doll," Lenny shouts and the uncles wave at me.

"Uh oh," I say but reach up to kiss Ryker before walking over to join the uncles at the table.

"What's up?"

"You need to settle a bet for us," Lenny says.

I'm afraid to ask. "What bet?"

"Which one of us is going to walk you down the aisle," Sid explains.

"Yeah," Wally says. "We know it won't be your sperm donor."

My eyes widen as I look around the table. Lenny, Barney, Wally, and Sid are all staring at me with hope in their eyes. Do they *want* to walk me down the aisle?

"Um." I bite my lip. "I got engaged this morning. I haven't thought about the wedding yet."

Sid snorts. "I know women. They have elaborate weddings planned long before they land a man to marry."

"You may know women, but you don't know me. I have no idea what kind of wedding I want."

The one thing I am one-hundred percent sure of is it won't be a big affair. My marriage to Theodore was the event of the year. My wishes weren't taken into consideration at all. Theodore and my mother hired a wedding planner and my opinion was not needed. It definitely wasn't wanted. I don't know why I was surprised considering I didn't have a choice of groom either.

Barney snickers and rubs his hands. "Sid's out. He doesn't know our Phoebe."

I expect him to start shouting *pick me, pick me* at any moment.

Pops comes out of the kitchen carrying a large ham. "Food's ready. Take your seats."

I sigh in relief and take my spot next to Ryker.

"Besides, if any one of us is walking Phoebe down the aisle, it'll be me," Pops declares before returning to the kitchen.

I bury my hands in my face. I'm never going to hear the end of this. "Maybe we should elope."

Ryker chuckles as he places his arm around my shoulders. "If you want to elope, we'll elope. But, just saying, I want a wedding."

What? I remove my hands to look over at him. "You do? Are you going to wear a tux?"

He shrugs. "I don't care. I'll wear whatever you want me to wear."

"But a wedding? Like in a church."

"Again, I don't care where we get married, but I want to get married in front of all our friends and our family."

He said it again. *Our* family. My eyes burn, but I won't let the tears fall. I don't want to ruin Christmas by sobbing all over the food. But I can't stop my lips from trembling. Ryker leans down and sips at them until the urge to cry subsides. I take a deep breath and return my attention to the table.

"Why is no one eating?"

Suzie rolls her eyes. "Duh. Because we're too busy staring at the scary dude go all gentle when he looks at you."

I have no response. Everyone's attention moves away from me and my fiancé when Leroy starts barking and pawing at Suzie's chair.

She reaches down to pick him up. "Poor baby. Is no one paying you any attention?"

The dog licks her face before scrambling out of her arms right onto the table. He races to the platter of ham and snatches a slice before running to the other side of the table where he hops onto a chair before jumping to the ground.

"Let him have it," Hailey says as Aiden scoots his chair back to stand. "And you know where you're sleeping tonight."

"Yeah, yeah. The doghouse." He marches off after the little thief.

"Your holidays sure aren't boring," Grayson says as he looks around the table with wide eyes. "But I don't think I want a slice of ham now."

Barney raises an eyebrow. "You aren't afraid of a little puppy saliva are you, soldier?"

Oh great, another ex-solider. Just what we need.

Suzie's sitting across from me with her head lowered. She's staring at Grayson from under her lashes while biting her lip.

Her cheeks are pink and I'm pretty sure I see longing in her eyes.

I was wrong. Maybe an ex-soldier is exactly what we need.

D. E. Haggerty
Love and Laughter in Every Chapter

About the Author

D.E. Haggerty is an American who has spent the majority of her adult life abroad. She has lived in Istanbul, various places throughout Germany, and currently finds herself in The Hague. She has been a military policewoman, a lawyer, a B&B owner/operator and now a writer.

www.ingramcontent.com/pod-product-compliance
Lightning Source LLC
LaVergne TN
LVHW010317200726
843507LV00010B/1264